Embracing the Consequences

Ravager Knights MC Book 3

M.E. Thornwood

Midnight Dreaming Publishing

Midnight Dreaming Publishing

P.O. Box 312 Elburn, IL 60119

Interior design by Atticus

Book Cover by Covers by Jules

Edited by Maine Woods Editing

ISBN 978-1-962688-05-5

ISBN 978-1-962688-04-8 (ebook)

EMBRACING THE CONSEQUENCES is book three of the Ravager Knights MC series. This is final book in a series where the previous books must be read before this one.

This is a Why Choose novel, meaning the main character will not choose between her love interests. This novel has BDSM themes and on page negotiations.

This book contains rough sex, praise and degradation, kidnapping, psychological torture, pregnancy, and angry alpha males that fly off the handle. If this is not your cup of tea, please don't read. This is a work of fiction intended for an 18+ audience.

Bikertok...

...lets bring on the Harley guys.

Chapter One

T HERE ARE PIVOTAL MOMENTS in a person's life when you can dynamically feel that your life is about to change, that past this one moment in time, *everything* will be different...forever.

Sometimes those moments pass by us without a thought: finishing a favorite book, the end of an anticipated vacation.

Then there are the moments when you pause and recognize explicitly that *nothing* will ever be the same: graduating high school or college, moving to the other side of the country, starting a new job.

Or the death of a family member.

The death of Mac "King" Taylor, president of the Ravager Knights Motorcycle Club, hit Kara's family hard. The news had plowed through their lives that day and left a shitstorm of chaos in its wake.

Mac Taylor had been a king in his own right: a leader, a friend, a president, a father, a damn good man. Kara knew the Ravager Knights MC would never be the same after his passing, just as she knew the lives he touched would never be the same. His death left a hole inside both the club and his loved ones, a hole that would never be filled.

As Mac was president of the national charter of the Ravager Knights, the funeral had been pushed out a week to allow time for members from every charter across the US to travel to Mourningside, Illinois. It would be an epic showing of colors, brothers from across the nation banding together in this time of grief.

Kara might have only met the man once, but even then, she knew he was larger than life. She heard it in the stories men told when they were deep in their drinks at night. She heard it in the way the old ladies spoke about him with a bit of reverence in their voices. She saw it in his son every single day.

Kara found herself at a loss for how to help Johnny since Mac's passing. So she did the only thing she could do: she wrangled the old ladies to handle meals and lodging for the club. Even though they had a full restaurant and chef on hand, they had closed things down to family only.

Sheila, Hotrod's wife, was a godsend in organizing all the women and showing Kara the ropes. Spare rooms were turned over, sheets cleaned, cots set up. She made sure everything was ready for when the hordes of out-of-town charters descended on the clubhouse.

Kara took her cue from Sheila, letting her take charge. She supposed that now that Johnny would be the new president, as his old lady, that duty should or would fall to her...but Kara hadn't thought about those ramifications yet—they'd technically only been dating three months.

They had been three fast and glorious months. But she knew in her heart it didn't matter. She'd told Johnny as much before. He'd moved her into his house when hers had burned down, and they'd agreed she was staying for good. Somehow that had only been six weeks ago.

They hadn't been home much in the week since Mac was killed in jail by Las Serpientes, a rival gang. Kara stayed at the clubhouse with her boys: Derrick "Devil" Halson and Kevin "Rockstar" Adams. They ended up in Johnny's room most nights since it had the most space and the bigger bed, though that didn't really matter. Though Johnny never left the clubhouse, he didn't come to bed with her and his brothers. Most of the time it felt like he avoided her at all costs.

Kara would get up in the middle of the night to look for him. Some nights she'd find him in his father's room, sitting in his recliner and just staring into space. Other nights she'd find him in his father's office or church, staring into space. One night she found him in the garage, working on his father's '79 Camaro.

That night—almost a week ago—was the last time Johnny had spoken to her. She'd tried to get him to come to bed, and he'd brushed her off. They hadn't argued, he had just told her he'd come to bed when he was ready before he turned his back on her.

She tried to not let it get to her, tried to be strong for him when he was around. But late at night, when both Derrick and Kevin were sleeping on either side of her, she let the tears fall. She hated that he was hurting so badly. She wished he would let her help him.

The funeral was in two days, and the clubhouse was busier than ever. Sheila brought back the caterers and restaurant staff: it was all hands on deck to feed the army of men that descended on the clubhouse. Kara was glad to hand over the reins to the professionals.

With the meals taken care of, there wasn't much left for Kara and the women to do. Most of the girls sat back and drank—if they weren't pregnant like Marlie and Rachel—with their men.

Kara found herself feeling out of place.

Johnny had made it clear he didn't want to be around her. As vice president of the Ravager Knights, Johnny was next in line to take over upon his father's untimely death. An official vote hadn't happened yet, and wouldn't until after Mac's funeral, but it was more a formality at that point. Johnny was busy making his rounds with his brothers. Though he wasn't talking to her, he was at least talking with them.

During the day, Kevin was also busy making the rounds with the out-of-town members who rolled in daily for the funeral; since he was the likely choice for vice president, it was expected of him. With Johnny tapped to be president, it would be his job to appoint the new vice president. Derrick had told her not that long ago that Kevin was a shoo-in for the role. Kevin, who had been Johnny's best friend since childhood, had grown up in the club alongside Johnny. Their fathers had been best friends. It made sense.

Kara knew it did, but she hated the pressure it placed on Kevin's shoulders. She hated that Kevin had lost some of his cocky swagger since Mac's death. He'd always had a mischievous glint in his eyes that drew Kara in. That glint had dimmed in the last week.

And Derrick, well, he kept her company when he could, but as the club's sergeant at arms, he was busy digging into Las Serpientes, looking for a weakness and for a way to stop this war before it could kick off completely.

There was no doubt that Mac Taylor's murder had left a void. They'd lost a giant in their world. Together they would have to carry the weight of his legacy.

Kara just wondered if she would still have a place in their new world.

AS DUSK FELL ON the clubhouse the evening before the funeral, Kara packed up the last of her things from Johnny's room. Derrick told her they would be giving his room to an out-of-town president. Derrick and Kevin were also giving up their rooms in the dorms to accommodate the sheer number of guests they now hosted. The club had rallied to find beds for everyone. Between brothers' own homes and dorm rooms and the motel down the street, they had made it happen for the over three hundred members.

Kara was in the process of loading her Lincoln MKX when she felt Johnny watching her. She glanced over her shoulder to see him, half in the shadows, some twenty feet away. He was leaning against the wall of the clubhouse, his foot propped up, while he smoked a cigarette, the red-orange cherry burning in the night. The shadows hid his face, but she knew he was watching.

He was always watching. His eyes had tracked her around the clubhouse all week. Constantly watching. He just never approached her. He made no move to come to her now either.

She sighed and tossed her pillow on top of her duffel in the back of the SUV. She had somehow managed to acquire quite the collection of personal items at the clubhouse in the last week. When she was done, she hit the button on the tailgate and stepped out of the way of the automatic closing gate.

She turned to Johnny. He was still there, cherry glowing in the shadows, though now his entire body was cloaked in shadow. She thought about ignoring him as he had ignored her all week, thought about getting in her car and driving away. But in her heart, she knew he was hurting and wasn't handling things well.

She approached him slowly. He might not have been talking to her this week, or even coming around her much, but he had yet to push her away.

She stopped a foot or so away from him, unable to see much of his face past that burning cherry. She hated that he'd resorted to smoking again. He had quit for years, but the stress of the last week had him picking up the habit again. "Hey," she said softly, unsure of where she stood with him. She hated this distance between them.

The only answer she received was the flare of the cherry.

"I'm gonna take off. Your sisters are at the house, and Derrick said you were giving your room up for the next couple days..."

When he still didn't respond, she grew frustrated. "You know what Johnny? I'm trying to be understanding here. I'm trying to give you space. You don't need to be a complete dick about it and ignore me when I'm talking to you," she snapped, taking half a step toward him. She understood needing space, but being an asshole and straight up ignoring her when she spoke to him? She wouldn't stand for it.

His answering growl was the only warning she got before he flicked the cigarette away, an arch of sparks as it sailed through the air. Then his hands were on her upper arms as he grabbed her and spun them around, slamming her back against the wall.

Her breath left her in a whoosh, but Johnny didn't give her a moment to recover. He was on her, pressing her against the brick wall with his leather-clad body. His hand wrapped around her jaw as his mouth claimed hers. She held onto his leather cut for dear life as he poured all his pent-up emotions, everything he had been hiding and holding back from her, into a kiss so breathtakingly passionate it left her gasping.

She soaked it up, sucked his tongue into her mouth, slid her hands up his chest and wrapped them around the back of his neck. His own hands slid down her waist and to the backs of her thighs.

He picked her up effortlessly, and she wrapped her legs around his waist.

She was desperate for him; the ache between her thighs burned for him. She moaned when he nipped at her lower lip. She dug her fingers into his shoulders and swiveled her hips against his.

He gasped into her mouth, then was moving quickly. He unbuckled his belt and the button on his jeans, pushing his pants down just enough to pull out his very hard cock. Kara was never so grateful that she had opted to wear a skirt that day, hoping to soak up the last of the summer days as September inched closer.

Now she was grateful for the easy access as Johnny slid her thong aside and pressed in slowly. She was shocked by his slow thrust. She was sure from his demanding kiss and his manhandling of her that she would be in for a wild ride.

He broke their kiss. He pressed open-mouthed kisses down her jaw till he got to her neck, to that sensitive spot just below her ear, the spot that was hard to cover unless she wore a scarf. That's where he laid his brand. He thrust his hips slowly, while he marked her.

She was a panting mess. All she could do was hold on tightly while he fucked her senseless. She was well aware of the fact that they were only a handful of feet away from the main party outside the clubhouse, where the picnic tables and makeshift firepits were set up. Her MKX was parked out front, under the big lights, in front of everyone.

She came on a low moan as her body shuddered and her walls quivered around his cock. He grunted as she clamped down on him, and he picked up his pace, finally pounding into her as she thought he would from the start. He came a moment later, his hips stuttering against hers, his breathing ragged as he groaned and finally lifted his mouth from her neck.

She could feel the bruise already formed there; he'd sucked so hard she was sure it would take weeks for it to heal. She didn't care, not in this world, where that claiming mark was all that stood between her and an out-of-town idiot who might not know who she was. She'd wear Johnny's mark like the badge of honor it was. She was his and he was hers.

She held him to her while they caught their breath. She didn't know what she expected to happen after that quick lovemaking session, but she hoped he'd at least talk to her. When he didn't say anything and slowly pulled away from her, she felt cold.

Tears prickled her eyes, and she tried to blink them away, hating that he wouldn't speak to her. He pressed a soft kiss to her lips before fixing her thong and setting her down gently. He buttoned up his jeans and fastened his belt while she smoothed down her skirt. Then he grabbed her hand and laced their fingers together.

He pulled her away from the wall, around the dark corner they had hidden in, and into the brightly lit parking lot. She felt eyes on her the moment they started for her Lincoln. There were easily a hundred people loitering around outside.

Johnny didn't say a word as he led her over to the driver's door of her SUV. He pressed her against the side of her MKX and, using his forefinger, gently lifted her chin to look up at him. His blue eyes were dark with pain. She hated that look in his eyes, hated that he seemed to be saying goodbye to her.

"Johnny." She breathed his name out softly, so only he could hear. She was well aware of every eye on them, wondering where she stood with their president. Women wondered if they could make a move on her man now that he was president, even if it wasn't official. Men wondered if she was a club whore or his old lady. She ignored them all and slid her hands up his chest and around his neck.

He cupped her chin gently between his thumb and forefinger before he lowered his lips to hers. The kiss he placed there was gentle and sensual before he slid his tongue into her mouth, turning it filthy.

She gasped and opened for him, ignoring the eyes on them, on her. He broke the kiss a moment later. He looked sad as he stared down at her. "I love you," she murmured softly, needing to say the words.

He sighed and pulled her into his arms, hauling her off the side of the MKX and engulfing her in his embrace. She wrapped her arms around his waist and rested her forehead against his chest, breathing in his scent. His usual sandalwood and leather were now mixed with the scents of nicotine and tobacco.

He pressed a kiss to her forehead before he pulled away. She reluctantly let go and put on a brave face, knowing damn well every single woman gathered was watching. She had to put on a brave face and be strong. Be his old lady.

He opened the driver's door for her, and she climbed in. Once she was buckled up, he leaned in and pressed one last lingering kiss to her lips before he stepped away and closed her door.

It wasn't until she had driven halfway home that she it occurred to her that he hadn't spoken a single word.

When she woke up alone the following morning, she realized that things between them had changed. A pivotal moment in their relationship, and she was left alone.

Chapter Three

T HE GATHERING FOR KING was the largest funeral pro-
cession the club had ever seen. As the national charter's
president, he'd been the king of all Ravager Knights. Now
that he was gone, his absence left a void that nobody could
completely fill.

Johnny could only *try* to be half the man his father had been.

He knew he wouldn't come close. His father had been such
a larger-than-life person he could command attention just by
walking into a room. He'd earned the respect of every single
brother in the Ravager Knights MC.

That respect was evident when each and every single member
of their charters from across the nation showed up in force. Over

three hundred in total, well more than they had projected and well more than their restaurant and wait staff could handle.

Kara had taken one look around at the chaos and immediately jumped on her phone. Within an hour, she had every food truck in the county lined up in the back lot of the compound. She organized bounce houses and face painting for the kids, she found hotels and motels for the additional guests, she brought in a live band and a DJ for music, she hired caterers and bartenders and busboys. She even set up the guest rooms at Johnny's house for his own sisters and coordinated their transportation from the airport.

Everywhere he turned, there was something Kara had organized. She had worked with Sheila and the old ladies on the dorms and had organized his guys to set up outside the clubhouse, transforming the patio area. Firepits and extra chairs had been brought in. She had completely transformed the compound to house and entertain everyone.

And she had done it without complaining...or Johnny's speaking to her.

He frowned when he realized he hadn't spoken to her in over a week. She had stopped trying to reach out to him. She threw herself into helping the club, his brothers, the old ladies. Anywhere she could help, she worked. He watched her when she was busy. He saw how his family loved her, how she fell right in with the old ladies without a hitch. His Knights were eating out of the palm of her hand. She never had to ask them twice to do anything.

His brothers... Johnny could see the shift in Kevin already, the impending vice president patch weighing on him. Even Derrick had been more subdued in his joking and playing around. Thankfully Derrick was keeping a close eye on Kara since Johnny and Kevin had their hands full.

The day of King's funeral, Johnny pulled up to his house for the first time since his father had died. He'd been sleeping on the couch in his father's office or the garage all week. He'd showered once, midweek, at his office for Taylor Construction. He had gone to check in on projects and his team there. Thankfully Taylor Construction was a well-oiled machine with enough project managers and foremen that work was always moving, whether he was there or not.

Johnny was surprised when he pulled into the garage and neither Derrick's nor Kevin's bikes were there, but he hadn't asked them when he saw them at the clubhouse. Kara's MKX was there, beside his truck, though. Johnny headed into the house and was surprised by the quiet. Usually Kara had a TV on or music playing when she was home alone.

He didn't see either of his sisters either. He knew they'd gotten in late the night before. They had both started blowing up his phone asking him when he'd be home. He had to tell them he was busy with the club because the thought of going home had his stomach in knots.

The house was eerily silent, but it was early still, so maybe everyone was still sleeping. Johnny headed upstairs and paused outside his bedroom door. He took a deep breath, steeling himself. He knew she would be pissed at him for not speaking to her for over a week, for shutting her out completely.

He pushed open the door and found the bedroom empty. The bed was mostly made, aside from the left side, as if Kara had slept alone in the king bed. He frowned, turning his head to look down the hall, as if he'd see one of his brothers in their bedrooms.

Then he heard it: the telltale sound of retching coming from the master bathroom. He stepped into the bedroom and headed for the bathroom just as another round of retching started.

Johnny paused in the bathroom doorway.

Kara was on her knees in front of the toilet, her hair in a messy bun. Short black cotton shorts and one of Derrick's gray T-shirts covered her. Her skin was pale and sweaty, and she had deep circles under her eyes. She looked like she hadn't been sleeping. Both tattooed forearms were braced on the toilet as she leaned over the bowl.

It hit him then, what he was seeing: the cast was gone. The bright pink cast that had been completely covered in art and signatures from friends and family was *gone*. Her right forearm looked slightly skinnier than the rest of her arm, even from a distance.

She hadn't noticed him yet. When he stepped into the bathroom, his heavy boots slapping on the tile, she startled and spun his way. She quickly reached for toilet paper and wiped her mouth before she flushed the toilet.

"You OK?" he asked, stepping toward her, worry creasing his brow.

She ignored him and stood up slowly. Her legs shook under her as she pushed herself to her feet. She reached for the counter just as her legs wobbled violently.

Johnny lunged quickly. He wrapped an arm around her waist as she caught herself against the counter. "Kara," he muttered, staring down at her.

She was breathing hard, but she wouldn't meet his gaze. "I'm fine," she muttered before she turned on the faucet and bent over to rinse her mouth out.

"Are you sick?" he asked, stepping back to give her some space.

"I'm fine," she repeated, a hint of anger laced in those words.

Johnny sighed and stepped back another step. She was pissed off at him, he knew. She had every right to be upset with him; he had essentially shut her out for over a week.

He watched her brush her teeth in silence. He didn't know what to say, didn't know why he hadn't been able to talk to her all week. He didn't know what to say about anything. He knew she'd have questions—questions he couldn't answer.

His father was killed by a gang hit that was ordered by a rival club. It had been set in motion by Kara's father. He didn't know how to talk about that with her, he didn't know how to talk about that with anyone, really.

He sighed and turned toward the shower. He needed to wash up and get dressed and then head back out...hopefully with Kara riding with him. He started the shower and turned back toward her. He didn't like this awkwardness between them, didn't like the distance. They were oil and water on a good day, but when they were at odds, Johnny didn't know how to act.

He let the water heat up and turned toward Kara. She was watching him in the mirror. Her eyes were red rimmed, but he could see her damn lawyer mask slammed down and locked in place. That stoic mask had pissed him off so many times in the course of the last three months. "Kara," he murmured before he stepped toward her.

Her eyes flashed in warning. She quickly bent over the sink and spat her toothpaste into the sink. He moved slowly, gave her plenty of time to rinse out her mouth and wipe her face before he stepped up behind her.

He wrapped his arms around her and pulled her back against him. She leaned on him and rested her hands on his forearms where they wrapped around her shoulders and chest. When she didn't speak, he realized she was waiting for him to say something.

"When did you get your cast off?" he asked, wondering if he'd been so out of it all week that he hadn't noticed. He sure as hell hadn't noticed when he'd loaded her into the driver's side of her

MXK. After six weeks of not being able to drive due to the damn cast on her right hand, he should have realized she was driving.

"Yesterday." She spoke softly. "Marlie took me."

Johnny sighed and closed his eyes; he held her tighter and took deep steadying breaths. Her messy blond hair smelled like vanilla and caramel, like her, sweet and comforting. Like she usually was. She put up a great front. She was a hard-ass on the exterior, but she was sweet like candy on the inside, and he hated that he was killing her by pushing her away.

"I'm sorry I wasn't able to take you," he murmured, keeping his eyes closed.

Her hands squeezed his arms gently, but she otherwise kept quiet.

"I'm sorry I've checked out this week," he whispered, feeling guilty.

Kara finally let go of his arms. She turned in his embrace, and he slid his hands down her body and wrapped them around her waist instead. He rested his forehead against hers, feeling the tears well up behind his closed eyes.

Kara wrapped her arms around him just as the sob tore out of his chest. His body shook, and he clutched her to him tightly, needing that lifeline. To him, she was the most important thing in the world. She was the love of his life, and he needed her more than air.

His knees buckled as sobs tore from his chest uncontrollably. Kara lowered them to the bathroom floor. He held her to him, pulling her into his lap as he cried on her shoulder.

She held him as tightly as he clutched her. Her hands rubbed his back, his shoulders, his buzzed head. She murmured soft words of comfort and rocked him slowly. She was his light in the darkness, his anchor in the storm, and he hoped she never let go.

Chapter Four

KARA EVENTUALLY SLID FROM Johnny's lap as his sobs slowed and his breathing calmed. "Let's get you showered," she murmured softly and grabbed his hand. The shower was still running, probably cold by now, but they both needed to wash before the long day ahead of them.

She helped him to his feet and gently started undressing him. She started with his cut and carefully laid it on the bathroom counter, showing it the respect it deserved. Then she moved to his hoodie and shirt, helping him pull them over his head. She let his clothes fall to the floor, not worried about them.

His fingers were slow, and he fumbled with his belt, as they still shook slightly. She gently pushed them aside and undid his belt and jeans for him, the ones he had been wearing the night before. From the smell of him, he'd probably been in the same clothes for a couple days.

It was no matter. She crouched down and reached for the laces on his boots, pausing as a wave of nausea rolled through her. She had to breathe through it to concentrate on the task before her. She had a long day ahead of her; she would have to pack some crackers to nibble on throughout the day.

"How's your knee?" Johnny asked as she pulled off his boots.

She shrugged. "It's alright. Physical therapy is down to once a week starting next week. I have exercises I do at home, but it's mostly strength training at this point. I'll see the PT for a couple more weeks just to make sure I'm not reinjuring anything, but I'm mostly in the clear there. But with the cast off my wrist... I start PT on that twice a week next week."

"So still three days a week?" he asked wryly and moved toward the shower.

She followed him in. "Nah, they'll roll the knee appointment into one with the wrist and I'll only have to go twice a week."

Johnny nodded and slipped into the water stream. He hissed and adjusted the temp.

"Cold?" she asked, a soft smile on her face.

He shook his head. "Hot. Tankless hot water heater, remember?"

Her eyes widened, and she moved closer to him, feeling the water. "Babe, we have multiple showerheads in here." He motioned to the one behind her that hadn't been turned on.

She shrugged. "I want to be close to you," she murmured.

His bright blue eyes darkened with desire, and his hand shot out and wrapped around the side of her neck. He hauled her against him without saying a word. The kiss that followed was pure *need*. Kara was glad she had brushed her teeth when she did. She still worried he might taste something unsavory on her tongue, but by the intensity of his kiss, there was nothing to worry about.

She closed her eyes and gave herself over to the kiss, wrapping her arms around his neck and pressing her naked body to his as warm water cascaded down from the rainfall showerhead.

Johnny's hands were like iron on her hips as he hoisted her up. She wrapped her legs around his waist as he pressed her back into the cool tile. He didn't waste a moment of time, lining himself up at her entrance and sliding home. She groaned into the kiss and arched her back. She was still sore from their time together the night before against the wall of the clubhouse.

Johnny growled into her mouth as if he was thinking the same thing. He broke the kiss and kissed down her jaw to the very purple hickey he had sucked into her skin the night before. "Fucking *mine*." He growled before he bit down on the tender flesh of her neck.

She cried out, her walls fluttering around him. Shock slammed through her at how quickly she had orgasmed. The pain of his bite was such a stark contrast to the pleasure the orgasm had torn out of her. "Johnny." She panted.

"Every fucking person today is going to know exactly *who* you belong to," Johnny growled into her ear.

"Yes, sir," she agreed, barely able to hold onto his shoulder as he fucked her harder.

"You've been so fucking good this week," he stated, his voice rough. "I've been watching you: organizing the old ladies, the caterers, the activities for kids." He fucked her while he spoke, each thrust punctuated by his words. "You've shown everyone how you're the top bitch around here."

Pride flared through Kara. She didn't think she'd done anything any one of those girls wouldn't have done for the club. She'd stepped up and taken charge. Sheila might have shown her the ropes, but by the end of the week Kara had run the show. She didn't think it was a big deal, but Sheila had told her that everyone was watching. All eyes were on the president's old lady.

The courtesans, the club whores as they were called, had kicked back a little bit in the beginning, but Kara was used to busting men's balls in the courtroom all day, every day. She wasn't about to take shit from the club's sluts. They quickly fell in line and did whatever she asked.

"I want you by my side today," Johnny commanded, his voice like gravel in her ear. "All day, not a step away from me."

Kara gasped, and Johnny pulled away from her neck to meet her gaze. His blue eyes were raw, the emotion unfiltered. Her heart broke at the pain there. She nodded slowly, wondering why he suddenly was feeling so possessive. "What's going on, Johnny?" she asked softly.

"I—" he shook his head. He stopped thrusting to look at her. "There's going to be a lot of outsiders there today. Most will see you with me and leave you alone, but others will see that you aren't inked as my old lady. You don't wear the Ravager Knights ink," he explained. "Some might see that as an opening."

Realization dawned on her. He was worried she would be in danger from his own club members, those from out of town. "Johnny," she murmured, wondering where he was going with all this.

He swiveled his hips, keeping his cock in the conversation. "I'm not making any declarations today. I love you. You know I love you, right?" He cupped the side of her face and brushed his thumb along her cheekbone.

Tears welled in her eyes as she nodded. "Yes, Johnny," she whispered. "I know you love me. I love you too." She pressed a kiss to his lips.

He smiled sadly. "I know we've talked about you staying here, and I want that. But this life, the club, it's not something to be taken lightly. I know it can be *a lot*, and we've got time after all the shit settles with your dad and this fucking war." He growled softly.

A shiver ran down her spine.

"We're going to have that conversation: about the club, our life, our plans, our future," he promised, his eyes blazing with intensity as he stared into her own sky-blue eyes.

A sob tore out of her as her tears fell freely. "Ink me today, baby," she whispered thickly. "It doesn't matter to me. Today or months from now, it doesn't change a damn thing for me. I choose you. I choose us. I choose you, and Kevin, and Derrick. I choose this life we've built together in the last three months. I'm all in. I told you already, I'm not leaving. You'll have to throw me out if you want me gone."

A growl tore out of him before he captured her mouth in a filthy kiss that stole her breath away. She clung to him as he snapped his hips against her and resumed fucking her. She held on, arms wrapped around his neck, and enjoyed every moment of his rough touch. "Fuck, baby." He groaned, his hands palming her ass, spreading her cheeks apart.

His fingers slid forward and gathered the slick from her pussy and slid back to her puckered hole. She groaned when he slid a long finger into her back passage as his lips caught hers again. She arched against him, needing to mark him as much as he was marking her. She broke the kiss and pulled him down to her. Her lips latched onto his neck, and she nibbled and sucked her own mark into his skin, managing to place it right above the armored knight he had tattooed there.

She gasped as he slipped a second finger into her ass.

Johnny lifted his head and gave her a cocky-as-fuck smirk. "I'm gonna tattoo your name right there," he declared.

Her eyes widened at his meaning: the spot on his neck where she laid her claiming mark. "Johnny!" She cried out as another orgasm tore through her body. "Fuck." She gasped as she went boneless against him.

"Goddamn, Kara." He growled as her walls clamped down on him and milked his cock. "I fucking missed you." He rode her through her orgasm before he fell over the edge himself. "Fucking hell." He grunted as he spilled his load inside her.

They were both breathless and panting, and Kara wondered how Johnny was still standing after all that. She slowly released her legs from around his waist, and he gingerly lowered her back to the ground.

Her knees only wobbled slightly as they accepted her weight. Johnny pressed a kiss to her forehead before he turned back to the shower. They washed quickly. They had a long day ahead of them, and there wasn't much time left until they had to go.

Kara dressed in a black halter style corset top with a leather skirt and knee-high boots with a six-inch heel. She teased her hair a bit at the roots to add volume to her big, luxurious curls. For her makeup, she went with a dark smoky eye and a deep red lipstick.

Her tattoos ran from her shoulders down to her wrists. Everything that could easily be hidden behind clothing for work was out on proud display today. She had more on her torso and thighs. Her largest one was a continuation of the black and red roses and skulls on her arms that ran down her right side and down her right thigh to her knee. It was clearly visible under the pleated leather skirt that came to midthigh.

"Holy fucking hell." Johnny groaned from behind her.

Kara looked at him in the mirror as she was putting hoop earrings in her ears. She took in his dark blue jeans and black button-down shirt and the black tie under his Ravager Knights leather cut. He already had on a pair of mirrored sunglasses and a black baseball hat worn backward. He looked hot as fuck and cleaned up well.

She turned and faced him slowly, letting her eyes drift up from his heavy biker boots to the jeans that hugged his thighs. The black button-down was untucked but still molded to his muscular chest.

His thumbs hooked into his pockets, the rings and tattoos covering his hands on display. A hint of a watch peeked out from his left sleeve.

"You look like a sexy badass biker." She grinned, moving toward him.

"That's why you love me, isn't it?" He smirked down at her.

Butterflies danced in her belly and her heart pounded in her chest. This cocky-as-fuck man who constantly got under her skin always had a way to get her going. "Yep, 'cause you look pretty," she shot back at him.

"At least I've got that going for me," he muttered and slid his hands around her waist as she drew closer.

She slid her hands up his chest and around his neck, grateful to be cast-free. She leaned against him and gave him a sad smile. "How are you doing?" she asked softly.

Johnny sighed and shook his head. She couldn't see his eyes behind the mirrored sunglasses, and she had a feeling he'd worn them on purpose. "Not good, babe. Not good."

She sighed and nodded. "I'm here for you. Whatever you need."

"I need you by my side today, no wandering away. In front of all the charters today, you are *my* old lady. As the soon-to-be president of the national charter, I need to be seen as strong. With that comes a strong old lady, do you understand?"

She frowned. "Kinda. So many already know that you share me with Kevin and Derrick, though. Is that going to change?"

He shook his head. "That won't change. I know you started this with Kevin. I know you two had something first, but this has grown to be more among the three of us. I don't want that to change. I won't let that change, OK?"

"OK," she said slowly, still trying to wrap her head around what he was really saying here.

"But today," he sighed, running his hand over his hat-covered head, "today, all eyes will be on me, son of the national president, VP, and soon-to-be new president. I need to be seen as strong and unflinching. Unmovable. Does that make sense?"

She nodded and slid her hand from around his neck to rub over his bearded cheek. "You've gotta be seen as impenetrable, even within your relationship with me. Top of the world with no one able to come between us."

He nodded and pressed a kiss to her lips, a soft, gentle, chaste kiss. "For today, try to keep the PDA with Kev and Derrick to a minimum. They should have been here to explain it too, but I've dropped the ball this week with you with all the shit in my head."

"Hey," she said, shaking her head. She ran her hand along his jaw again. "Don't beat yourself up. Your dad was murdered, it's not your fault. You have every right to be in your head. I'm honestly surprised you're even able to be with me after what my father set in motion." She sighed, looking down.

His arms tightened around her waist. "You have nothing to do with your father. I love you, and that isn't going to change because your father is a piece of shit." He growled.

She smiled faintly, trying to ignore the tears welling in her eyes. She took a deep breath and willed them away. "I love you too. I'll be by your side all day, and tomorrow we'll talk about everything else. OK?"

He nodded and leaned down and pressed another soft kiss to her lips. "I don't deserve you," he murmured against her lips.

"Yes, you do. Come on," she muttered, patting his chest and slowly pulling back from him.

# Chapter Five

K EVIN "ROCKSTAR" ADAMS STOOD outside the clubhouse with Derrick and Hotrod. It was early in the morning still, but Kevin hadn't been able to sleep. He felt like shit for leaving Kara alone at home. He hadn't gone home the night before, and when he'd run into Derrick half asleep in a recliner in the lounge, he'd realized that Kara was home alone.

Around four a.m. Kevin had finally gone into the garage office and kicked the couch that Mayhem was passed out on. Johnny had startled awake, but Kevin didn't care; someone needed to be at home with Kara. It wasn't safe for her to be alone, not with Las Serpientes and the Devil's Psychos making moves against the

Knights. And Johnny had all but ghosted Kara all week. It wasn't fair to her.

It had taken some time to get Johnny up and out of the clubhouse, but once he'd finally left, Kevin replaced him on couch to catch a couple hours of rest.

Now that he was standing outside the clubhouse, around one of the many firepits that Kara had thought to bring in, he was upset that he hadn't gone home himself. He would have loved to wake up with his woman wrapped up in his arms, her curvy body pressed against his. He had been a damn fool for staying the night before.

"Here he comes," Hotrod murmured, nodding toward the gates.

The men manning the gates moved and opened them quickly as Johnny rode through them with their girl riding bitch. "Hot damn." Derrick groaned, eyes on their woman.

Kevin couldn't blame him; she looked fucking hot as hell. Her blond hair was down and full of big sexy curls. Her eyes had dark make up that made her bright blue eyes pop vibrantly. The red lipstick though? Fuck him. He'd love to see those pouty red lips wrapped around his cock. Maybe he could sneak her away at some point in the day.

As soon as he had that thought he knew he couldn't. Not today at least, not with every damn charter here for the funeral. With the vote later and Johnny possibly taking the helm as national charter president, Johnny was under the microscope today. He would need a strong woman by his side, one who wasn't shared with his brothers, even Kevin and Derrick, at least for the next couple days.

Once their visitors left, they could go back to normal. Kevin just wished he had spent the night at home, wrapped around his woman, so he didn't feel so lost now that he had to keep his distance.

Kara slid off the bike, and Kevin groaned. She wore a leather jacket over a halter style corset top and a fucking leather skirt with knee-high biker boots. She was fucking gorgeous. She knew her role today and chose an outfit to fit that—add in the two sleeves of tattoos and she was one badass babe. She was going to be a damn fine Head Bitch in Charge of the old ladies.

"You boys going to be OK today?" Hotrod asked, his voice soft and gruff as he stared across the lot at Johnny and Kara.

"Gonna have to be." Derrick sighed, his eyes on their girl.

Kara took a step away from Johnny so he could swing his leg over the bike. Once he was standing, he grabbed her hand and headed toward the three of them standing at the firepit just outside the clubhouse.

Kara ran her eyes over Derrick and Kevin, briefly noting Hotrod standing with them, as she walked over, hand in hand with Johnny.

"I'll give you guys a minute," Hotrod muttered before he walked away.

"Morning, Pres." Derrick's voice was louder than normal as the two of them walked up.

"Mornin'," Johnny answered gruffly.

Kara gave a tight smile, her eyes darting between Kevin and Derrick. "I wish you guys had come home last night," she said softly so only they could hear.

Kevin froze seeing the pain on her beautiful face. Shame and disappointment rolled over him. He had been an idiot for not going home to her last night. He shifted and sighed. "I know. I'm sorry," Kevin said softly, well aware that this was not the time or place to be having this conversation.

It may have been early in the morning, but there were still eyes on them. People were waking up and heading outside for their morning cigarette. Kevin hated that he couldn't wrap his arms around her today, hated that society as a whole had issues with polyamorous relationships even if they were becoming more mainstream every day.

"Me too." Derrick nodded solemnly.

"Tonight," Kara muttered.

"Tonight," Johnny agreed and pressed a kiss to her temple. Her sky-high heels brought her closer to his height, but he still towered over her.

Kara forced a smile to her face. She looked between Kevin and Derrick one more time before she turned with Johnny and headed into the clubhouse.

There wasn't a hearse towing their brother, their president, to his resting place. Instead, an all-glass carriage that looked like something out of *Cinderella* was towed by a trike driven by funeral director Nick Barrett, a biker himself and a friend of the club. The glass trailer behind the trike had been his idea several years ago when his own father had passed away.

It seemed like the club had used that carriage all too often since then.

Johnny and Kara rode directly behind the carriage—a lone bike in formation, the spot to his right purposely left open for the ghost rider that would have been Mac. Behind Johnny, Derrick and Kevin rode side by side. The rest of the club and their guests followed in a similar two-by-two formation.

Their caravan was miles long. They had paid the local police to escort and stop traffic as they moved through the city. Over three hundred patched members of the Knights had shown up to pay tribute to their fallen president.

Kara looked every bit the bad bitch that a biker's old lady should be. She sat proudly behind her man, arms wrapped around his waist, her blond hair flying in the wind. The corset she wore with that pleated leather skirt, paired with the tattoos and boots, was hot as fuck and showed off what Kevin already knew: she was a fucking knockout.

The ceremony at the cemetery was short and sweet. The priest, a friend of the club, gave a heartfelt eulogy remembering Mac. Johnny stood by and listened, his head down and sunglasses firmly in place, looking as stoic as he could save for the white-knuckled grip on Kara's hand.

Kara's tears surprised Kevin, though he didn't know why. Kara was as compassionate and empathetic as they came. She met Mac only one time, but that didn't matter because she knew what he had meant to all of them.

Kevin stood on Johnny's right hand, with Derrick to Kara's left, the two of them flanking their president and his old lady. The rest of their charter of the Ravager Knights stood around them, both flanking and surrounding Johnny, protecting him from danger even from within their organization.

After the priest was done, Mac's coffin was lowered into the ground. People threw flowers into the open grave. Some lingered to speak to Johnny, but most headed back to their bikes or vehicles.

Once Johnny and Kara were seated on Johnny's bike, Kevin revved up his engine. As road captain, it was his job to signal the bikers' tradition of ringing out the dead with *the last rev.* Soon, every single biker, over three hundred of them, was revving their engine in response.

A chill ran down Kevin's spine as he let off his throttle. One by one his assembled brothers released their own throttles, and the sounds of revving engines slowly faded away until the last one lone biker—the tail gunner—revved his throttle for the final time.

Chapter Six

Johnny looked around the clubhouse, taking in all his brothers and friends wearing their cuts with a new black and red patch sewn on, a patch with the skeleton knight now boasting angel wings. There were birth and death dates on the patch along with the words *In Loving Memory of Our King*.

Those not wearing the new patch had on a T-shirt or an armband with the same logo as the patch. Black and red was everywhere; even Kara had donned the red and black armband throughout the day. His heart had warmed knowing his woman had organized the memorial and ordered the massive quantities of memorial pieces.

He glanced around the room again, looking for Kara. She had stayed by his side all day and evening, had been his rock throughout, only leaving his side to go to the bathroom or grab him a drink. Now that it was going on midnight and he was ready to head home, he couldn't find her. She had said she was going to the bathroom, but that was ten minutes ago. After sweeping the room again, he headed toward the bathrooms in search of his old lady.

Cracking the women's restroom door, he heard her retching before he saw her. He frowned; had she been feeling sick all day? He'd thought she'd been feeling better. Why was she still out if she wasn't feeling well?

"Kara," Johnny heard Rachel sigh, "have you seen a doctor yet?"

Johnny stopped dead in his tracks. There was a short hallway before the turn into the main bathroom. He was out of sight for now, but he wasn't sure why he was hiding.

"No." Kara groaned, her voice cracking. "I called, but they won't see me until eight weeks. I'm only six weeks along," she muttered. "I made an appointment. They gave me a list of shit to not eat and meds to stay away from." She let out a shuddering breath.

"Did you tell them how sick you were?" Rachel asked.

"They didn't seem to be too concerned, said it was normal. If I can't keep down any water throughout the day I can call back. But really, it's just smells that seem to set me off." Kara's voice grew stronger the longer she talked.

Johnny's heart pounded in his chest, his thoughts whirling a million miles an hour. And yet, he couldn't seem to comprehend what he was hearing. Was Kara *pregnant*?

"Have you talked to your guys yet?" Rachel's voice was kind and gentle.

"No." Kara sighed. "I only realized something was up a couple days ago. Shit's kinda been crazy lately. I figured I'd tell them this weekend. Hopefully we can get some time alone."

Johnny closed his eyes and took a deep breath. Kara was pregnant. *Fuck.* He could feel life as he knew it coming to a halt. He was standing at a crossroads, and only he could choose the way forward. Was he ready to be a dad? He had no idea. But he knew in his heart Kara was it for him; there was no other option.

He made a show of opening the bathroom door before he shouted into the bathroom. "Kara? You in here?"

"Yeah," she called back. "Give me a minute and I'll be right out!"

"Alright. Slade's ready for you. Meet me there." He turned and headed for the corner where Slade had set up shop.

Slade Cooper was the club's go-to tattoo artist. She had a shop on the border of Mourningside and Creekton. She'd also been a friend of Kara's for years and had done all her ink. She'd set up fabric partitions to separate her space in the back corner from the main barroom. Behind the curtains there were a couple chairs, a couch, and a table where Slade was organizing her supplies. "You got time to do that one we talked about?" he asked her.

Slade's eyes widened as she looked up at him. "Now?"

"Absolutely." He nodded.

"Yeah, for sure."

Johnny paused a moment and asked quietly. "Is it safe to ink if she's pregnant?"

Slade gasped; her vibrant green eyes went wide. "You mean?"

Johnny nodded. "She doesn't know that I know yet, so don't say anything please. She hasn't told us yet, but I heard her talking to Rachel," Johnny admitted.

"Holy shit." Slade gasped. "Congratulations?" she asked.

Johnny grinned widely and nodded. "Thanks. You can see why I want her inked tonight, if possible?"

"Yeah. Holy shit," she muttered, clearly floored by the idea.

"So is it safe?" Johnny pressed again, looking toward the bathroom door.

"Yes." Slade nodded. "The biggest concern would be infection, but we're using medical-grade sterile equipment, and Kara isn't allergic to my ink. She'll be fine."

Johnny nodded. "Alright. Let me grab my brothers."

Slade smiled and quickly started pulling out supplies. Johnny turned and found Kevin and Derrick in the crowd easily enough. Both men had kept an eye on him all night. It wasn't hard to get their attention and motion them over.

"It's time," he told both men when they stood before him.

Kevin's subtle intake of breath had Johnny eyeing him. "What's wrong?" Johnny asked his brother.

"Are you sure? You were just sworn in as president two hours ago. You want to go public with this right away? I thought we were going to wait."

Johnny shook his head. He eyed the bathroom, still not seeing Kara. "Things have changed. I'll fill you in at home," he said, giving both Derrick and Kevin a slight shake of his head. "But I want her inked. Now."

Derrick opened his mouth to say something but quickly closed it.

Kevin eyed him suspiciously. "I thought we were going to ask her together?"

"We still can." Johnny sighed. "I just want her inked tonight. So, you got some grand gesture you wanna do or say? Have at it. But before we leave here, our names will be inked on our girl's body."

There was a small feminine gasp, and Johnny looked over Kevin's shoulder to see Kara standing there. She was pale. Johnny could see the exhaustion etched on her face. Her eyes were red rimmed, like she had been crying, though her makeup was fresh. He could see the hints of purple beneath her eyes, the exhaustion there, though she'd tried to hide it. He hated that she was so sick and so tired.

"Come 'ere," Johnny murmured, crooking his finger.

Kara moved toward him slowly, her eyes wide. She looked so fucking beautiful. Her blond hair was still in curls, though they were a little windblown and flattened from the long day.

"Johnny," she murmured, eyes watering.

Johnny sat down and pulled his girl down on his lap so she was straddling him. He wrapped his arms around her waist and pulled her close. He caught the scent of mouthwash on her breath and pressed a kiss to her lips. "We had planned on taking you out, doing this right, but I don't want to wait any longer. I love you. *We* love you." He motioned to Kevin and Derrick. "We want you to be our old lady. Officially. If you'll have us?"

Tears poured over her lashes as she nodded and let out a laugh. Her smile grew wider as she wrapped her arms around his neck.

He pulled her against his chest tightly. He never wanted to let her go. He pressed a kiss to her lips, and she smiled against him. "Let Slade tat you? Then she'll ink the three of us with your name. Then we're going home."

Tears slid down Kara's face as she nodded and kissed him again. He slanted his mouth over hers and slid his tongue against the seam of her lips. She tentatively opened for him, and Johnny slid his tongue inside, caressing her tongue with his. She tasted like toothpaste and mouthwash. He groaned, knowing she was carrying his child, their child.

Johnny's hand slid from her hip to her belly and lay flat against it. "I love you," he murmured softly.

Kara's hand found Johnny's, and she laced their fingers together over her belly. "I love you too," she murmured. Her eyes bounced back and forth between both of his, as if she were trying to read between the lines. She turned from him to look up at Kevin and Derrick. "I love you both, so much." She gave them a watery smile.

Derrick leaned down and pulled her into a passionate kiss, his tongue licking into her mouth only inches from Johnny's face. "I love you too, baby girl," he murmured against her lips.

He stepped back a pace to make room for Kevin.

Kevin was rougher with her than Derrick or Johnny had been. His fingers curled in the back of her hair, and he pulled her head back so he could claim her mouth. She moaned as he bit down on her bottom lip.

She shifted in Johnny's lap, and he groaned as he grew hard beneath her. "I love you too, babe," Kevin said softly as he pulled away from her.

She smiled, half in a daze. "What do you want inked on me?" she asked.

"Slade already drew it up this week," Johnny answered, nodding toward the black-haired woman.

Kara looked over her shoulder at her friend to see her holding up a drawing. It was a red and black ink design of the Ravager Knights skeleton in armor. It was riding a Harley while holding a blood-dripping scythe. Red roses and thorns were wrapped around and through the knight, and in a fancy script around the knight were their road names: *Mayhem, Rockstar, Devil*. Above the image, in an arc was *Old Lady*.

Kara gasped when she saw it. She stood from Johnny's lap and turned to her friend. "It's amazing." Her hands shook as she reached out and ran her fingers over the design. "Where do you want it?" She looked up at Kevin and Derrick.

"I was thinking here," Johnny replied, as he stood up. He rubbed the back of her right shoulder. Her upper back was free of ink, and the image was large. It would cover one whole shoulder blade.

"I agree." Kevin nodded. "When you wear a tank top, it would be on display."

"I think you should also get our real names somewhere on your body," Derrick suggested.

"I agree." Kara nodded and turned to Slade. "I want their names, their real names, right here." She ran her fingers across the tops of her breasts.

"Fuck, baby." Johnny groaned and ground his hips up against hers.

She smirked and pressed a kiss to his lips.

"It's late. You want me to do all that tonight?" Slade asked. She didn't seem upset about it, she was just asking.

"Nah. Just do the old lady ink," Johnny answered. "We'll swing by the shop tomorrow for the rest."

"Sounds great." Slade smiled and gathered her tools.

In the end, Kara lay down on the couch and Slade worked on her shoulder blade. It took her about an hour from start to finish and created a beautiful mix of black and red ink that blended seamlessly with her older work.

Kara was half asleep when Slade finished, so the boys let her doze while they got her name tatted on their bodies.

Johnny kept his word and had her name tatted in a scrolling cursive script right over the hickey she'd made on the left side of his neck. It was low enough that a collared button-up shirt would mostly cover it, but he didn't care. He wanted her name where the world could see. She owned him, and he was proud of that fact.

Derrick did the same, tatting her name on his neck. It was the only place available for more ink at this point. But Kevin was the romantic. He tatted her name on his left pec, right above his heart.

Neither Derrick nor Johnny gave him shit about it. If it wasn't for Kevin, they never would have made a move on their girl.

Chapter Seven

T HE DAYS THAT FOLLOWED Mac's funeral passed in a blur. The other charters left the clubhouse and headed back to their homes. Kara went to Slade's shop, Skin of a Different Breed, and got her boys' names tatted right on the tops of her breasts.

She wore a regular spaghetti strap cami like the ones she normally wore under dress clothes to give Slade a baseline to work off. When Slade was done, a perfect long curved line in the same cursive script that Kara's boys rocked with her name spelled out all three of their names right across the tops of her breasts for the whole world to see.

She knew there were tops that she wore to work that would now show that new ink, but she didn't care. She wanted the world to know that these were her men. And she was theirs.

Kara spent the rest of the weekend either in bed or running to the bathroom to throw up. When Sunday afternoon rolled around, Kara was crying softly on the bathroom floor when Johnny walked in. She had just finished getting sick, hadn't had the chance to even brush her teeth yet, when he sat down on the floor next to her.

She briefly wondered why the two of them always ended up here together, why all of their major life-altering conversations happened in this bathroom. Something about the space calmed her, though. She only wished Kevin and Derrick were in the room, too, so she wouldn't have to repeat herself.

Because she knew exactly what Johnny was going to ask. He'd seen her puking up her guts for the last four days.

When he wrapped an arm around her shoulder and pulled her against him, she went easily. She leaned against him, feeling weak and lethargic. The sickness was getting worse, not better. She was barely eating. Most smells set her off, and what little food she managed to eat didn't settle right in her tummy. She even had problems keeping water down at this point.

"I made homemade chicken noodle soup," Johnny murmured softly as he ran his hand down her back.

She closed her eyes. "Thanks," she muttered. Her entire body ached; everything hurt. She was probably dehydrated too.

"I sent Derrick to the store to pick up some things."

"Mmm," she mumbled, not really paying attention. She was so tired, so weak, and Johnny was so warm. She wanted nothing more than to bury herself in his body and soak up his heat, his strength.

"Some ginger ale, crackers, Popsicles."

She didn't reply as her heart suddenly pounded in her chest, her thoughts racing a million miles an hour after his statement. She needed to get up and brush her teeth. She wanted to crawl back into bed but didn't have the strength to stand up.

Johnny kept talking softly, though. His voice was a gentle rumble over the top of her head. "When is your appointment?"

She froze but didn't have the strength to fight. "A week from Tuesday." She sighed.

He pressed a kiss to her temple. "Maybe we should call the doctor tomorrow and make sure everything is still in normal range?" he suggested, running his fingers through her ponytail.

She pulled away to look at him. He didn't seem upset, just worried. "You're not mad?" she asked.

He gave her a soft smile and shook his head. "Nah, baby. I told you, I love you. You're it for me."

She wanted to smile; the relief that flooded her would have made her smile if she felt better. Instead, tears prickled her eyes. "Do Derrick and Kevin know?" she asked softly.

"Yeah, babe," Kevin answered from the open doorway.

A sob broke out of her as she turned to see both Kevin and Derrick standing in the doorway. The latter had a plastic grocery bag hanging from his hand. Both men were watching her with worried smiles on their faces.

"I was going to tell you guys." Her voice was jagged as she sobbed.

Johnny pulled her back against his chest, and she went easily, falling back into him. "Shhh," he whispered. "It's OK. I overheard you in the bathroom with Rachel at the clubhouse. It's why I wanted you inked that night instead of waiting. I told these two when we got home."

She only sobbed harder against him. She'd wanted to tell them herself. Maybe in a cute way with a baby onesie or something? They'd never discussed kids, but in the last couple weeks they had talked about their relationship and their future. They all had agreed they were in it for the long haul.

Kevin moved into the bathroom and sat down on her other side. He grabbed her hand and laced their fingers together as he lifted them to his lips and pressed a kiss to her knuckles. "We love you, baby. We just want you to feel better and not be so sick."

She heard boots slapping on the tile before Derrick's big body crouched down in front of her. "Baby girl," he said with a smile. His fingers cradled her chin gently and turned her face toward him. "I'm ecstatic that you're pregnant, but we're worried about you.

Let's get you feeling better, then I can show you just how happy you've made me."

She finally cracked a smile and nodded slowly. "K," she murmured.

"Alright, let's get you up." Derrick nodded.

Together, the three of them helped her get slowly to her feet. She brushed her teeth for the hundredth time before they helped her back into bed. Someone had changed the sheets, and she was grateful. She only wished she had taken a shower before she crawled in. Maybe later, she thought as she curled up on her left side.

The bed dipped behind her as someone climbed in, and she dozed off. She would deal with the ramifications of their conversation after she woke up.

She woke several hours later feeling a little better. She was warm and felt rested, not so weak and lethargic. She rolled over and was greeted by the sight of Derrick's bare chest. His torso was covered in tattoos, and when she looked up at him, she could see the fresh ink on his neck with her name.

She smiled and let herself admire the rest of him. His green eyes were closed, and his chest rose and fell gently and rhythmically. He was still sleeping. She was grateful for that. She had learned his breathing patterns in the week after he had been shot. Had that only been a few weeks ago?

She felt like time both flew and stood still the older she got. She never realized it as a kid, but it was both unforgiving and healing in a way.

She ran her hand over the scar that the bullet had left behind in Derrick's bicep. He had gotten extremely lucky that it hadn't hit him in the chest. Things might have ended so differently.

Fingers slid through her hair, and she closed her eyes, savoring the touch. In the days since Mac's funeral, the guys had made sure to be home every single night, but she still felt starved for their touch, like there was distance between them because she had been hiding this secret from them, holding herself back from them.

The bed dipped behind her as someone rolled over. "Fuck man," Kevin grumbled. "We need a bigger bed."

"Yeah," Johnny agreed from somewhere behind her. "I'll call that store tomorrow. See if they can deliver this week."

"Were the headboard and frame trashed at Kara's?" Kevin asked.

"Everything was soaked so the wood might be trashed. I can build a frame and headboard though," Johnny mused.

"We need to talk about remodeling and picking a room for the baby," Kevin added.

"We've got plenty of space. The baby will probably stay in here for the first couple months. But then we'll probably want them next door," Johnny said.

Kara's heart swelled as she sleepily listened to her men plan for their future. The love she felt for these three men was insurmountable.

"We'll have to put a fence around the pool." Derrick's voice rumbled, his chest rising and falling beneath her head.

"Yeah, shit," Johnny swore. "We better get a list going. We've got a lot to do."

"Guys, we have time." Kara chuckled softly. "But I'm not opposed to a bigger bed."

"Fuck yeah," Derrick added.

"I'll call tomorrow, reorder what we had before," Kara said.

"How are you feeling now?" Kevin asked as he rolled over and spooned up behind her.

"I'm doing alright right now. I have to pee and want to shower, but I'm feeling a lot better," she answered honestly. "Maybe a little hungry?"

"I'll heat up the soup. You shower," Johnny ordered, and she felt the mattress shift again as he rolled out of bed.

She yawned and mumbled her agreement but didn't move. She was comfortable, and for the first time in a while, her stomach wasn't rolling and cramping. She didn't want to tempt fate quite so soon but knew she needed to eat.

Eventually her bladder won out, and she detangled herself from Derrick and climbed out of bed.

After she got clean, she put on fresh jammies and headed downstairs to the kitchen. It was almost six, and the sun was just going down outside. Besides calling the shop for a new Alaskan king bed for the four of them in the morning, she didn't have much to do now that the case was officially turned over to the DA's office.

She was still on a leave of absence from Carmichael and Associates due to her supposed car accident, but it had been six weeks, and her doctor had cleared her.

"When does physical therapy start for your wrist?" Johnny asked as they sat around the breakfast nook eating homemade chicken noodle soup.

"Tuesday. I'll go Tuesdays and Thursdays. I'll probably schedule them for the afternoons since I can drive now," she said.

"So what are your plans during the day?" Derrick asked.

"I was thinking about going back to work. I'm still technically managing partner. I'm gonna call the board tomorrow and see what they say now that my father has been indicted and my doctor's cleared me for light duty." She looked around at the three of them.

To her surprise, none of them looked that upset at the thought of her returning to work. She'd imagined she'd be fighting an uphill battle with them, but Kevin gave her a blinding smile. "So I get to see you in the halls again, Boss Lady?"

She laughed. "I'd say so."

"How long will physical therapy last this time?" Derrick asked, looking pensive.

"Another six weeks." She shrugged.

"I don't really want you alone." Johnny spoke up after a moment of silence.

Kara looked up from her bowl and furrowed her eyebrows. "Why?"

"Your father is still out there. We know he's tried to kill you once. What's to say he won't try again? Especially now that he has nothing to lose because he already lost it." Johnny's voice was steady as he watched her.

Kara froze, spoon halfway to her mouth. She hadn't thought about that. When her father had skipped town, she'd thought that would be the end of it, at least until he was caught by police.

"I like the idea of you at the office because there's a lot of people around there. Good security, plus the three of us are there most days," Johnny explained. He took a deep breath and leaned back in his chair as he continued. "I want one of us still to go with you to physical therapy, just in case. I'd rather you just not go anywhere alone, period, until he's caught."

Kara sighed, but nodded, giving in. "Alright." She wasn't happy about it, but she understood the safety reasons behind it. Until her father was caught, she wouldn't put anything past him. Not after he'd already tried to have her killed once.

Her boys relaxed and smiled as if they'd been in a fight themselves.

She grinned and slowly ate her soup. She took sips of Gatorade in between, hoping to replenish electrolytes while she felt better.

She spent the rest of Sunday night nestled on the couch among her three men, some action movie on the TV while she dozed in and out, grateful to be keeping food down.

Chapter Eight

M ARCOS SAT IN THE barroom of the Devil's Psychos club-house with his two best friends, Jason "Stone" Langford and Nico "Dagger" Gage. Both men were nursing beers while they waited for the rest of the club to show up.

Church was scheduled for 10 p.m. It was already 9:50, and the key players were nowhere in sight.

"Watch him be late," Dagger grumbled. His blue eyes met Marcos's and gave him a knowing look.

Marcos nodded slightly, already knowing how his buddy felt about the situation. Their president, Larry "The Butcher" Buckley, was a piece of shit and didn't give a fuck about anyone but himself. He'd make them wait all night for his ass to show up.

And he was probably getting his dick sucked down the road at the whorehouse despite demanding all members be at the clubhouse by ten for the meeting.

Marcos sighed and leaned back in his chair, settling in for the long haul. Things had been tense around the clubhouse ever since Buckley chose to start a war with the Ravager Knights without a club vote. There had already been one casualty; Buckley had shot and killed one of the Knights in cold blood.

Rachet had been a friendly acquaintance of Marcos's over the years. He'd often run into him at Skin of a Different Breed when he got ink done. The tattoo parlor was owned by Garrett Cooper, but most days the old man let his daughter, Slade, run the shop.

The shop was on the border between Creekton and Mourningside, and Slade was all about the money. She didn't care who she inked as long as they kept the peace in and around her shop. She claimed the one-mile radius around her shop as a neutral zone.

Everyone followed the unwritten rules and kept their shit locked down when going to visit the Coopers. Everyone knew they had the best artists around, and everyone wanted their ink to look good.

After Rachet's death, Slade declared she was no longer going to be inking any Devil's Psychos while they chose to war with the Ravager Knights. Slade had drawn a line. Rachet had been a good friend of hers, and she would "declare her loyalty to the Knights for as long as the Psychos continued this unfounded vendetta against the Knights." Her words.

It had caused another ripple of dissatisfaction around the clubhouse when Trick had gone to get some ink done a couple weeks ago. It had been right before the Ravager Knights president had been killed by Las Serpientes in County.

Only a handful of people knew that Buckley and Vince Carmichael had ordered that hit. Marcos, Stone, and Dagger were the only ones in the clubhouse that knew Buckley was responsible for the deaths of King Taylor and Rachet, killed on an ambush he had led while on a run in Alabama. When Marcos had confronted Buckley on that, he had gotten more lies and the runaround. "Saw an opportunity and I took it." Buckley had defended himself. He hadn't cared that it had started this damn war with the Knights. Hadn't cared that they almost lost one of their own for spying.

Now it was only a matter of time before the Knights retaliated.

And Marcos didn't know where that would leave him with his sister dating the new president.

Church turned into a clusterfuck. Marcos didn't even have to say a damn thing for it to unravel into a shouting match. The brothers were *not* happy with the new war and what it meant for their families.

It may still be a man's world among bikers, but men with wives and children knew they needed to keep them safe. And an unhappy homelife made for some cranky-ass bikers, regardless of how hard-ass they fronted away from home.

Trick and Ransom, a solid set of brothers who had been patched in for over a decade and best friends to boot, shared a look before they turned to Marcos and met his gaze. They gave him a subtle nod, and Marcos acknowledged them with the tiniest tilt of his head.

A quick glance at Buckley showed he was glaring across the table at Stone and Dagger, who had been arguing with one of the prospects loyal to Buckley.

It was a clusterfuck.

When Stone met Marcos's gaze, Marcos gave him a subtle shake of his head. Stone looked away quickly and trailed off, finishing his argument with Buckley. He must have kicked Dagger under the table because he, too, quickly trailed off.

Suddenly Buckley's raspy voice was heard over the last of the arguing. "I don't give a fuck about what this club thinks. I'm the damn president, and what I say is law," he spat at Dagger.

"That right?" Bear asked. He was one of the old-timers that had been best friends with Jerry Langford, Stone's father, and had always been an uncle figure to Stone, Dagger, and Marcos. He was a seasoned Psycho in his fifties and a no-nonsense kind of guy. His once-dark hair was graying at the temples, but he had it cut into a modern style with the sides faded. He still had a rock-hard body and worked out about as much as he drank each night.

He leveled a glare at their president. "This democracy going full-blown dictatorship?" he questioned, crossing his arms over his chest.

Buckley seemed to have realized what he said and tried back-tracking. "Now that's not what I meant to say," he stammered.

"The hell it's not," Bear shot back. "Your actions lately have spelled it out loud and clear. Since when do prospects sit in church?" Bear raised a heavy gray eyebrow at Buckley from across the table.

There was a rustling as brothers looked around the room. "What the fuck?" Nickle glared, looking around the table. The poor bastard was still recovering from the beatdown he'd gotten from the Knights. Besides bruises, a broken rib or two, and a broken nose, he was lucky to have been mostly uninjured after being caught spying on the Ravager Knights—on Buckley's order.

Marcos took that opportunity to speak up. "Grunts out," he ordered.

There was a painfully long pause as the five prospects turned to Buckley instead of listening to a direct order from a patched brother, their VP at that.

Marcos narrowed his gaze on Buckley as the man nodded to the prospects around them. The five men that Marcos didn't recognize stood up and filed out.

"I don't remember voting on any new prospects either. Let alone *five*," Marcos stated, his voice low. "Who the hell are they even? Who vouched for them?"

"Not me," Trick said.

"Me neither," Ransom shot out.

Bear, Nickle, Dagger, and Stone all shook their heads.

Before the door could close completely behind the five prospects, the door swung open again and four imposing figures filed in.

Fucking finally, Marcos thought as Ace, Axel, Blaze, and Phoenix filed in. They were followed a moment later by Jerry Langford. When the five men were seated around the table, Marcos made sure to look them each in the eye as he asked, "Where the hell were you guys?"

"Doing a job for me," Buckley shot at Marcos before any of the five men could answer.

Marcos watched them unfailingly though. There was something off about their disappearance. Marcos wasn't particularly close with Ace, Axel, Blaze, and Phoenix, but he would be questioning Jerry later, in private.

Ace glared at Marcos, and Marcos glared back.

Something was going on, and Marcos would get to the bottom of it.

Chapter Nine

J OHNNY ROLLED INTO THE parking lot of the hole-in-the-wall diner on the border of Mourningside and Creekton with Kevin and Derrick on his heels. The nondescript building was run-down, but Momma Jean served up a mean cup of coffee and had the best damn pancakes around.

Johnny parked his Harley up front in the lineup of three other bikes. He cut the engine and dismounted, setting his helmet on the handlebar and waiting for Kevin and Derrick to follow suit.

"You sure about this, man?" Derrick asked, scratching his thick beard as his green eyes surveyed the patrons through the windows.

Johnny couldn't fault his brother for the distrust. After all the shit that had happened between the Devil's Psychos and the Ravager Knights lately, Johnny was questioning his own decisions here.

They'd murdered Rachet, sent a spy to the clubhouse, teamed up with Vince fucking Carmichael, and ordered a hit through the fucking Las Serpientes on his own damn father. They'd killed his father.

By all rights, they had declared war on the Ravager Knights.

Johnny could have ordered them all dead, on sight.

Instead, he was meeting with Marcos Candela, the VP of the Devil's Psychos, in neutral territory. Momma Jean's was inside the Coopers' one-mile radius around Skin of a Different Breed. Momma Jean also had the same philosophy as Slade Cooper—no sides, no drama, just pay up. It made for a great meeting place when discussions were needed. It also helped that Momma Jean was a hard-ass who kept a twelve gauge behind the bar, and she wasn't afraid to use it.

Johnny nodded his head once at his brothers before he headed for the door. Kevin was already a step ahead of him and opened things up. He did a quick surveillance of the inside of the diner before he stepped out of the way and let Johnny through.

Johnny gritted his teeth at his brother's mother-henning, but it wasn't that long ago that Johnny was doing the same thing for his father. It was part of the job as the club's vice president. Johnny nodded his head at Kevin as he walked by him, noting both Stone and Dagger sitting at the diner's long counter.

Stone and Dagger were notorious in their own rights, but neither had ever personally done anything to slight Johnny. He nodded once at them and headed for the back corner booth where Marcos was already seated.

Johnny moved slowly, not happy that once he took a seat his back would be to the room, but as this was a show of *trust*, he would have to deal. He trusted his brothers to have his back should anything unsavory arise.

"Hey man." Marcos stood up and greeted Johnny as he walked up. He held out his hand and Johnny shook it. "I'm sorry about your old man."

Johnny paused, slightly off guard, but nodded. "Thanks." He shook his hand. "I'm actually glad you called."

Marcos eyed him, the mistrust evident in his dark eyes. "You are?"

"I know shit is fucked up right now," Johnny said with a sigh.

Marcos nodded warily and motioned toward the booth. They each took a seat, and Marcos shook his head. "I know you have no reason to trust me right now. Not after the shady shit with Buckley and Carmichael and your father." He sighed. "But I want you to know, I had nothing to do with it."

Johnny met Marcos's dark gaze with his own steely blue eyes. "I wouldn't be here if I thought otherwise," Johnny stated plainly.

Marcos nodded once. "Buckley's getting more unstable," he offered. "He's taken on five new prospects that no one's vouched for. He's going full-blown dictatorship. He tried to cover his ass when called out on it, but he doesn't really give a fuck."

Johnny leaned back in the booth and sighed. "That's not good news, brother."

Marcos jerked his head at the moniker, his dark eyes flashing with an emotion Johnny couldn't read. As quickly as it was there, it was gone. His VP mask was pulled back into place, a mask that Johnny was all too familiar with after being with Kara.

"And how is my sister?" Marcos asked, as if reading Johnny's mind.

Johnny smirked slowly. "She's great." He nodded slowly and rubbed a hand over his hat covered hair. "She's...uh...well she hasn't been feeling the greatest lately, but she's doing well. I'd expect a call to dinner one day." Johnny alluded to as much as he could. He knew Kara wanted to speak to her brother on her own. He and Marcos still had unfinished business between them, but he recognized his girl wanted to reconcile with her brother.

A hint of a smile tugged at Marcos's lips. "I see you made things official." He rubbed a finger on his own neck, indicating Johnny's new ink.

Johnny grinned broadly. "Yep." He nodded once. "Derrick and Kevin too." He nodded toward his brothers.

Marcos looked over to see the fresh ink on Derrick's neck, but Kevin's was hidden by a shirt. The vein in Marcos's jaw throbbed as he ground his teeth. Whether he was angry or annoyed, Johnny didn't know or care. "Kara wants this?" Marcos asked.

Johnny chuckled deeply. "You're already in hot water with your sister. You really want to ask me that?"

"Fuck." Marcos swore and shook his head. He ran a hand over his skull trimmed black hair and sighed. "Fucking hell."

Johnny nodded and motioned for the server. An older woman walked over with a pot of coffee and two menus. The men placed their orders quickly and flipped their coffee mugs for the woman to fill.

"I never wanted this life for my sister," Marcos said, pouring an obscene amount of creamer into the coffee.

Johnny eyed him amusedly; seeing the similarities between him and Kara was unnerving. "I wouldn't want this life for either of my sisters," Johnny placated the man. "Truth is, I tried to push her away. I knew she was too good for this life and had too much to lose, but at the end of the day, she fought for us as much as we fought for her. For some reason I can't fathom, she wants the three of us bastards, and we'd do anything to protect her. We love her, man," Johnny explained.

Marcos gave him a wry smile and shrugged. "She always did whatever the hell she wanted."

Johnny smirked. "I know that all too well."

After the initial posturing, things calmed down between him and Marcos. They ate their breakfast and discussed how to best take out Buckley. Marcos would first need to figure out who was loyal to him, but after, Johnny would take the matter to his club for a vote. If all went well, the Knights would assist in the removal of Buckley and gain retribution for not only Mac Taylor but Rachet as well.

When it was time to leave, both men stood up and grinned as they shook hands. "If all goes well, I'll be seeing you for dinner soon." Johnny nodded at the guy.

Marcos laughed. "Yeah, tell my sister not to poison me, will ya?"

Johnny laughed. "No worries there—I'll grill."

"In all seriousness," Marcos said, pausing before they headed toward their brothers, "I'm trusting you to take care of her. Keep her safe."

Johnny clapped a hand on Marcos's shoulder. "Trust me, *brother*," he stressed the last word, watching that flare of emotion cross Marcos's dark gaze again, "Kara will be under constant surveillance and kept as safe and sound as we can possibly make her."

Marcos nodded slowly, his mask falling back into place. "I'll hold you to that."

After breakfast with Marcos, Johnny headed across town to the Carmichael and Associates building. They had to pull over to remove their cuts and put them away in the saddlebags of their bikes before they arrived to the Carmichael building, but it was worth it to be able to see their girl back in her element. Taylor Construction was still working on the remodel of the building. His crew had made headway, his foremen taking over during his own absence.

Kara had started back at work that Monday, and while she said she loved being home with them, he could see how much she loved being back in the office. And Johnny loved watching her slip into her work clothes and don the air of Bad Bitch in Charge. It was hotter than hell, especially when he knew he could get her to drop to her knees and submit to him with just a word.

It was a powerful, heady feeling knowing that his woman trusted him that much; it made his heart sing. He would have to show her how much he loved her later that evening.

For now, the three of them dismounted and headed for the door near the loading dock. They had a long day of work ahead of them.

"I heard Vince hired someone to have her killed." A not-so-soft voice spoke behind Johnny and the guys.

Johnny's eyes narrowed on Derrick as they sat around a table in the moderately busy lunchroom.

The table behind them had been filled with people Johnny didn't know, and had no interest in knowing, until they spoke up.

"He tried to kill his own daughter?" someone else asked, their voice shocked.

"Yeah. That's what I heard at least. She apparently found that he had been embezzling from the firm. The news said she had to hand over hundreds of files to the DA's office," the first voice, a man, spoke up again.

Kevin was watching the table over Johnny's shoulder, his dark eyes narrowing in on the person speaking. He had worked at the Carmichael building the longest. He probably recognized faces and maybe even knew some of the people around them. Johnny would have to ask him later.

"I heard she was attacked in her own home," the woman gasped, clearly in shock. "But for her own father to have her attacked? That's a little far-fetched."

"It was outlined in the news report. You'll have to look it up," the man continued. "But the board brought her back on as soon as Vince was indicted. Apparently, he moved to have her terminated when he came back."

"Holy shit," the woman muttered again. "Goes to show you, blood isn't everything."

"Yeah." The man huffed out. "And now Vince is on the run and the firm is being investigated. How soon until Kara starts having security escort people out of the building? Or worse, the police start arresting people?"

"Well, I didn't do anything wrong, so I have nothing to worry about," the woman murmured.

The man made no comment.

"I heard they've already arrested Reid James, Jim Briggs, and Janet Walter. They were senior partners," another woman spoke up.

"No shit?" the first woman asked.

"Not surprising with how tight they were with Ken Laraway," the second woman said.

"I've already sent my résumé to a colleague at another firm. Might be time to make a move, before the house comes tumbling down," another man spoke up.

Johnny narrowed his eyes at that. Kevin met his gaze and shook his head. There was no use getting all worked up. This was bound to happen when it came to any kind of in-house scandal. He knew Kara was strong and could weather the storm, but it still bothered him to hear it in person.

He stuffed the last of his sandwich in his mouth and cleaned up his stuff. He had a sudden urge to see his woman and hoped her day was going better than the gossip he had to listen to.

By Friday evening after Kara's first week back to the office, Johnny was about ready to pull the plug on the whole thing. He hated her being away from them all day, hated that he went hours without laying eyes on her. He was seconds away from tying a damn tracker around her neck or locking her ass up in their bedroom.

That second idea had merit. He considered it, wondering how she'd handle some of their rougher play now that she was pregnant. It felt like he'd been googling the shit out of everything all week. He knew he wasn't alone in that whenever Derrick would spout off some random fact while they worked like, "She can't eat sushi anymore, but I can still eat her sushi," a typical crack that Devil was notorious for.

Johnny led the way into their house Friday night, Kevin and Derrick joking loudly behind him. He had a wide grin on his face, happy to be home, as he walked through the back door in the kitchen and headed for the kitchen table.

He looked around the great room and smiled wider when he saw Kara kicked back on the couch, her heels on the floor, and her stockings-clad feet up on the coffee table. Her formfitting dress had driven him crazy all day. The bright red chiffon or whatever it was clung to her golden skin. In the office, she had covered her tatted arms with a leather jacket that also hugged her curves. Now the jacket was draped over the back of a kitchen chair and her ink was on full display.

She looked so damn fuckable. "Fucking hell." Kevin groaned under his breath as he looked over at their girl.

She had a charcuterie board ladened with snacks on the table and three glasses of Macallan already poured. There was a wineglass of a clear bubbly liquid in front of Kara. She looked up from her phone when they walked in and smiled widely.

"Honey, we're home," Derrick greeted with a goofy grin.

"I can see that." Kara smirked.

Johnny took a seat at the table in the breakfast nook and made quick work of unlacing his steel-toe boots.

"Whatcha doing over there, pretty girl?" Kevin asked, bending down to unlace his own boots but keeping his eyes on Kara.

"Well since I can't drink wine..." she rolled her eyes, "I figured I'd pretend with some Sprite and you all could have a drink and relax...and maybe help me relax in return." She gave them a wicked grin.

"Fuck yesssss." Derrick groaned, ignoring his boots and stomping toward Kara.

"Derrick!" she snapped, her eyes wide and exasperated. "You're tracking mud everywhere!"

Devil didn't give a damn. He shot her a wicked grin before he launched himself at her.

She squealed in protest as he lifted her off the couch. He went to throw her over his shoulder and then realized last minute how fucking bad that would be. "Derrick!" she protested as he carried her bridal style toward the stairs. "Don't shake me so much! I don't want to be sick!"

Johnny laughed and shook his head at his brother's antics as the two of them disappeared up the stairs.

"Fucking finally." Kevin grinned. He stood from taking off his boots and made quick work of putting them in the small mudroom next to the back door.

"If dumbass doesn't give her motion sickness on the way upstairs." Johnny laughed. He followed Kevin's lead and put his own boots away before they headed up—following the trail of dried, crusted dirt—to join in the fun.

Kara's protests of "fucking mud all over my white carpet" were cut off midsentence, and a loud moan followed shortly after.

"Looks like he's starting quick." Kevin chuckled as he led the way to the master bedroom.

The scene they walked in on was right out of a porno. Kara lay on her back, skirt bunched around her hips, garter belt holding up her stockings and no panties in sight. Devil was face-first in her glorious pussy, already putting his mouth to work. Her fingers were tangled in his thick mane, her back arched and her breasts thrust forward. Her other hand was thrown over her head, and her eyes were squeezed shut. She was already panting from Devil's tongue.

She looked fucking fantastic.

Johnny knew he was dirty from work, though. He desperately needed a shower. He would have to clean up before he stuck his fingers, or his dick, inside their girl. Especially now that she was pregnant, they needed to make sure everything stayed clean down there.

Kevin had the same idea and headed for the shared master bathroom.

The new Alaskan king bed had been delivered the day before, cementing his brothers' move into the master suite. Johnny couldn't even be mad. It made their girl extremely happy to have all of them close, and he wouldn't complain about the extra sleeping space in the massive bed now taking up half the room like it had been meant to be there all along.

Johnny moved closer to Kara on the bed. She moaned louder as Devil really ate her cunt. Johnny smirked and slid his slightly dirty hands under her dress, groping her sensitive breasts.

She groaned and arched into his hands.

His thumbs slid across her nipples, making her moan. "There's a good girl." Johnny smirked and pinched her nipples. "Devil's eating that cunt right, huh babe?"

A breathy moan left her lips, and she gasped again.

"You going to be a good girl and come for us?" Johnny questioned again. He heard the shower start in the bathroom and wanted to move Kara's orgasm along so they could see her come before he took his shower.

He pinched her nipples roughly, and she whimpered as her back arched further off the bed. "Come for me, pretty girl," he ordered, his voice rough as he watched her face contort in pain before her mouth dropped open and she moaned loudly, her body shuddering.

Derrick held her in place and lapped and licked her through it.

"Fuck," she mumbled, her fingers tightening in his hair. "No more," she muttered, pulling at Derrick's hair.

He laughed darkly against her skin and shook his head against her pussy. "Never." He chuckled against her cunt.

Johnny smirked and tugged at her nipples. She arched again.

Kevin walked out of the bathroom completely naked and climbed on the bed with a smirk. "Go shower," he told them, then he dragged Kara up the mattress and away from Derrick's mouth.

"It's been too long since I've had this pussy." Kevin groaned and claimed her mouth.

Johnny left him to it and flew through the fastest shower of his life. The water had barely warmed up as Johnny attacked himself with a loofah. He made sure to scrub everything, though, not missing a spot. He wanted to be extra clean for his girl. The last couple of weeks had been rough for them, and he missed her too much to fuck this up.

When he was finally clean, he toweled off quickly and headed back into the bedroom. He smirked when he saw he'd beaten Derrick back. He must have gone to his bedroom to use his shower and save time.

Kevin was balls deep in their girl. He was on her, straight missionary, rocking into her slowly. She had her fingers laced in the hair at the nape of his neck and moaned softly.

"That's it, pet," Kevin said, his voice soft.

Kara moaned again.

"Such a good girl for us," he continued.

Johnny watched the two of them as Kevin took his time with her. He murmured words of encouragement to her. He brushed her hair back from her face reverently.

"Kevin." She gasped. She panted, her nails digging into his back.

Kevin reached up and grabbed her hand from behind his neck, pulling it over her head and pressing it down against the bed. "Both hands, pet," he ordered softly.

Kara listened beautifully, her submission always breathtaking to him. Her submission period was an earned blessing, but there was something special about watching her and Kevin together.

Johnny's cock was hard as a rail, but he ignored it as he watched his brother bring their woman to orgasm.

Kara arched against him, her hands held still by her own determination. She cried out, clenching and squeezing her eyes tight. Her body shuddered and writhed beneath him.

"Such a good girl," Kevin said as he gently moved through her orgasm.

"Such a pretty Princess when you come," Johnny said softly as he moved toward the bed.

Kara had a lazy smile on her face as she turned her head toward him. She slowly opened her eyes and gave him a wide grin before she turned back to Kevin and leaned up to press a kiss to his lips. She deliberately left her hands over her head on the mattress like he'd instructed.

"Are you done with me, sir?" she asked, a cheeky smile on her face.

"Not even close, baby." He smirked and pulled back.

"We're just getting started with you," Johnny added and climbed on the bed.

"You got that right," Derrick said from the bedroom doorway, where he stood buck naked.

"Thank fuck." Kara laughed. "I've missed this so much," she said, looking at Johnny.

"I know, Princess." He nodded slowly. He had built a wall between them in the last couple weeks.

"How are you feeling?" Kevin asked.

"So good," she muttered, twisting her hips.

Kevin groaned and thrust deeper into her. "Be a good girl and stay still," he said. He rolled them over quickly.

Kara gasped and braced her hands on his chest when she suddenly found herself on top of him.

"There we go." Johnny smirked and slid behind her. He ran his hands slowly up her sides until he cupped her heavy breasts in both hands. He kneaded and massaged them slowly, rolling her nipples between his fingers.

She moaned and arched back against him. She twisted her hips as she rode Kevin slowly.

He groaned and grabbed her hips, holding her in place. "You're fucking soaking my cock, baby." He gasped.

She smiled, and Johnny grabbed her jaw, turning her head and claiming her mouth, licking into her immediately.

The bed dipped as Derrick scooted in. "I could watch you for hours, baby girl," he said before he bent down and sucked a nipple into his mouth.

Kara gasped into the kiss, and Johnny pulled her lower lip into his mouth, sucking on it.

Derrick pulled away and grabbed the bottle of lube off the nightstand. He put it in Johnny's hand and pushed him away.

Johnny released Kara's lip with a groan and stepped away, making room for Derrick. Johnny lubed up his cock, then lubed up Kara's asshole. He slid a finger in and smiled when she pushed back against him and moaned. He slid another finger in and started scissoring them. He slowly worked her open as the bed dipped again and Derrick pulled her into a kiss.

Johnny didn't wait, using Derrick's distraction. He and Kara groaned together as Johnny slid into her tight passage, made even tighter with Kevin in her cunt.

Kevin groaned when Johnny twisted his hips, their cocks separated by only a thin layer of skin as they slid against each other.

"Come here, baby girl," Derrick said as he pulled away from their kiss. He wrapped his hand around the back of her neck and pulled her down toward his rock-hard cock. "There's a good girl," he crooned as she wrapped her lips around the head of his cock.

Kevin thrust his hips up hard, jostling Kara. She slipped and swallowed Derrick down further. "Fuck." Derrick groaned.

Kara moaned loudly around Derrick's cock, and it only spurned them all on. They set a steady pace, fucking hard but slowly. A deep, sensual drawing out only to snap back hard. She became a withering, whining mess among the three of them.

Derrick kept his hands on the back of her head and held her in place as he fucked her mouth.

"That's it, Princess, come for us." Johnny panted as he felt her walls clenching around him and Kevin.

"Fuck yes," Kevin groaned.

Kara moaned loudly around Derrick's cock as she came so hard her whole body shuddered with it.

"Fuck." Derrick gasped and groaned loudly as he stopped thrusting in her mouth and came.

Johnny wasn't far behind. "Fucking hell, Princess." He groaned as he came.

Kevin snapped his hips up as his fingers gripped Kara's hips. "So fucking good for us," he mumbled before he came with a low groan.

Kara collapsed onto his chest as Derrick pulled away.

Johnny pulled out slowly and went to the bathroom to clean up. When he came back out, Kara was still lying on top of Kevin. Johnny laughed softly. "Come on, pretty girl. You need to clean up. Then we should eat that snack you set out downstairs."

Kara yawned and said, "Bring it upstairs. We can watch TV in bed."

"Good plan." Kevin smiled and rubbed her back.

Chapter Ten

S ATURDAY NIGHT KARA PACED around the kitchen, stirring sauce on the stove and then checking that the place settings at the table in the breakfast nook were up to her standards. She had invited her brother to dinner earlier in the week, hoping they could mend their relationship and talk shit out.

Things had been tense between them ever since their argument months ago, before her attack. She had called him for one of their regular catch-up calls, and she had admitted that she was actively dating three men at the same time. He hadn't taken it well and all but called her a whore.

The shit at the beach and discovering he was a Devil's Psycho hadn't helped. Not only had he lied—or omitted the truth—her whole life, he was in the damn rival MC that was actively raging a war against the MC her men were in.

Add on the shit his president was doing with her own father, plus finding out that Marcos shared a father with Johnny, along with the death of Johnny's—and Marcos's—father, and shit had been strained between Kara and her big brother for too long.

She hated it. She missed her big brother.

She needed the evening to go well and was trying to make everything perfect. It was bad enough that she was attempting to host this dinner while *fucking sober*. She wondered how long it would take her brother to notice she wasn't drinking. She had money on ten minutes.

Kevin was the optimist and said he wouldn't notice. *Hah. Not the way he homes in on me the minute he sees me.*

Derrick had said after dinner and Johnny had voted for sometime during the meal.

Kara rolled her eyes. She knew her brother; he was a fucking hound dog and would sense something was off with her right away. So she poured a can of Sprite into another wineglass and hoped like hell it would buy her some time.

"Baby, you gotta relax. It'll be OK," Kevin said as he walked into the kitchen. He slid in behind her as she stirred the spaghetti sauce.

"Marcos and me..." she shook her head and trailed off. "We're oil and water on a good day."

"Nah, babe. That's me and you." Johnny smirked as he walked into the kitchen, blond hair still wet from a shower.

Kara grinned and let her eyes roam over her man. She took in the black T-shirt that hugged his muscular body and the blue jeans that hung low on his hips. His feet were bare, and for some reason she found that hot as hell. Domestic and homey. His blue eyes sparkled as he watched her check him out.

She gave him a smile as he leaned in and pressed a kiss to her temple.

It felt like a lifetime ago that she'd first met Johnny when he came to her office to present plans for the remodel. He'd shown up while she was in the midst of firing Ken Laraway for sexual harassment. She had thought he was hot but arrogant as hell. She'd been angry and worked up from dealing with one chauvinist dickhead; she didn't want to deal with another.

And while Johnny had proved himself otherwise, that initial meeting would always stand out to her. Especially as they had almost fucked in her all-glass office.

Now she didn't mind Johnny's arrogance so much. They weren't so much oil and water as they were oil and vinegar, went great together, often separated—butted heads—but were easily mixed back together—had amazing makeup sex.

In three short months, her life had completely changed. It had been seven weeks since her attack that had her moving in with her boys and set her on the case of the century, but she wouldn't change any of it for the world. Her ribs may still twinge from time to time, and her knee would swell and ache more than she liked, but she was healing. Her cast was gone, her wrist would get stronger, and her cuts and bruises were healed.

And most important of all, her heart was full. "I love you guys," she said and turned into Johnny's body. He wrapped his arm around her waist as she leaned into him.

Kevin came up behind her and grabbed her hand. He pressed a kiss to her knuckles. "I love you too," Kevin said. His deep, soulful brown eyes gazed down into hers with all the love in the world.

"Me too, babe," Johnny murmured and pressed another kiss to her temple.

"Is it love hour?" Derrick's deep voice rumbled from across the great room as he walked down the stairs. His hair was wet from a shower, his long, dark mane brushed and air drying around his shoulders, his thick beard still damp. He, too, had on a black T-shirt and blue jeans and was also barefoot, though a pair of socks was thrown over his shoulder.

Kara smirked. "Sure is, Devil boy. Come tell me you love me."

Derrick growled and moved quickly across the large room and into the kitchen. "I'll do more than that, baby girl." He ran and fell to his knees and slid across the wood floor. He came to a stop right at her feet.

She grinned wickedly down at him. "I like you on your knees before me."

He growled and lifted her shirt and placed an open-mouthed kiss on her belly before he bit down.

She gasped and threaded her fingers through his mane.

"You'll pay for that comment later, baby girl," Derrick said before he tugged her leggings down and licked through her folds.

"Fuck." She groaned and leaned back against Johnny and Kevin.

As if of one brain, both men reached out and pinched one of her nipples. She moaned again and jumped when there was a loud knock on the front door.

"No," she whined, panting slightly already. "Fuck." She groaned. "Fuck you guys," she grumbled and pushed away from her men. How the hell was she supposed to have an adult conversation with her brother when she was all fucking worked up?

She heard the loud smack to her ass before the pain registered.

"Keep talkin' back, Princess, and you're gonna regret it later." Johnny growled.

She shot him a smirk over her shoulder and headed for the door, straightening her clothes as she went. When she got there, she turned her back to the heavy wood door and faced her men; they were watching her suspiciously. She smirked and quickly lifted her shirt and bra, flashing her bare tits.

"Fucking beautiful," Kevin groaned.

"I'm putting you over my knee later, slut." Johnny growled.

She laughed and fixed her clothes. "You'll have to catch me," she taunted him before she flung open the front door and revealed her older brother, Marcos, standing on their front porch. His dark hair was buzzed short to his head, and his deep brown eyes were warm as a smile formed on his lips at the sight of her.

She gave her brother a bright smile and moved in for a hug. "Hey, Marquitos."

"Lil *Manita*," Marcos murmured and pulled her in tight. "Thanks for inviting me."

She smiled against his shoulder. "Thanks for coming, brother. It means a lot to me," she said as she slowly pulled away from him.

He was dressed like her guys, a plain back T-shirt and blue jeans, no cut in sight. She saw his bike in the driveway, though, so she assumed his cut was tucked into a saddlebag, because she knew her boys didn't leave home without it, ever. Even on the job, it was tucked into their bikes or trucks.

"I'm sorry again, about everything," Marcos said softly.

She sighed and hugged her brother again. "I know Marky Marc, I know. Me too."

He hugged her tightly again, and she leaned into him. At the end of the day, she missed her big brother. She loved him fiercely and hated not speaking to him.

She led her brother into the house. He pulled his boots off by the front door and walked through the great room in his socks. "Beautiful place you got here," Marcos said as he looked around at the vaulted ceilings and wooden beams stretched across from the second floor.

"Thanks, man." Johnny greeted him. He held out his hand and Marcos shook it. "Beer?" he offered.

"Yeah man, sounds great," Marcos agreed.

Kevin and Derrick also went over and shook Marcos's hand, welcoming him into their home.

Kara grabbed her wineglass of Sprite and prayed like hell that Marcos wouldn't notice she wasn't drinking whisky.

It was as if she thought it into existence, though. Marcos turned to her and raised an eyebrow. "Where's the whisky?" he asked.

She shrugged and took a sip of her drink.

"Since when do you drink white wine?" Marcos continued, not even realizing he was pressing her.

She rolled her eyes, annoyed. "You don't know everything about me, big brother. I enjoy white wine once in a while."

He barked out a laugh. "The hell you do. You tolerate reds in restaurants because of your snooty ass father. You're a whisky girl to the core, like I damn raised you. Is that even wine? You got Sprite in that glass?"

Her boys cracked up.

Kara blushed and covered her face. "Jesus fuck, Marcos!" She groaned and shook her head.

Marcos actually sounded confused. "What?" he asked.

She lowered her hands and looked up at her brother, exasperated.

"Is it really Sprite?" he questioned.

She sighed and nodded slowly. "Yeah," she deadpanned.

His heavy brows furrowed together. She could see the thoughts flashing across his eyes. For as much as he tried to be a masked hard-ass, he was still her big brother, and she could still read him like a book.

She watched when it clicked in his soulful brown eyes. She watched the warmth drain from them as his jaw flexed and he ground his molars, the vein in his jaw ticking. Then his eyes snapped shut and he took a deep breath and let it out slowly through his mouth.

He opened his eyes, and she once again saw the warmth there, the love he had for her. "Are you pregnant?" he asked slowly.

She bit her lip tentatively and nodded slowly. She could see her boys hovering behind her brother, but she kept her gaze on Marcos. She was nervous about his reaction and afraid he might not approve.

A smile cracked Marcos's lips, though, and she found she didn't have any reason to worry. "Fucking Christ," he swore before he swooped in and lifted her into a massive hug. He swung her around in a circle, laughing. "Congratulations lil *Manita!*"

Tears sprang to Kara's eyes, and she clutched her brother's shoulders tighter. "Thanks, Marquitos," she whispered.

"This is a good thing, right?" He looked over at her boys as he set her back down in front of them

Her men grinned and nodded. "Unexpected but to be expected." Kevin grinned.

"To be expected...'cause you're fucking three dudes." Marcos groaned.

Kara laughed. "Yeah. After the attack, between the painkillers and life being crazy, I never got my birth control refilled, and yeah..." Hearing it out loud, it sounded extremely irresponsible. But at the end of the day, she honestly had forgotten all about it.

"Are you happy, though?" Marcos asked.

"Ecstatic, brother," she answered with a bright smile. And she really was. "Now that I'm no longer feeling sick all day long."

"Morning sickness?" he asked, running a hand over his buzzed hair.

"All day sickness. To the point these guys were pretty worried," she admitted, motioning to the three men at her back.

A hand slid across the back of her neck and pulled her toward them. She saw Kevin out of the corner of her eye as he leaned in and pressed a kiss to her temple. "We called the doctor, but they stated it was normal, and by yesterday, she was starting to feel better," Kevin said.

"But it was pretty rough for the last two weeks," Derrick answered, surprising Kara. She hadn't realized that he had noticed the first week. That was the week of the funeral. They'd all been so busy she wasn't sure anyone had noticed her sneak off to the bathroom to be sick throughout the day.

"And you're all OK with this?" Marcos asked, looking among her men.

"Yep." Johnny nodded, a smile on his lips.

"Can't wait to see this belly all big and round, carrying my child," Derrick answered, pushing Kevin out of the way and wrapping his arms around Kara from behind.

Marcos shook his head at the display, but a smile was still on his face. "And you're all OK...sharing?"

"Just something we've always done." Johnny shrugged. "They're my brothers. It works for us."

"So will you find out who the father is?" Marcos asked.

Kara swallowed thickly and looked to her guys. Derrick's arms squeezed tighter around her.

"It doesn't matter to us," Kevin answered easily. "We're all gonna raise that child in this house and be fathers. Doesn't matter whose kid it is. The baby is ours."

Tears welled in Kara's eyes. They had talked about it—she had questioned them to exhaustion in the middle of the night when she couldn't sleep. Her guys had already made it clear to her that they didn't care, but it was still nice to hear it again.

Marcos turned to Kara with an unreadable expression on his face. "And you're happy?"

A broad, beaming smile lit her face, tears still lining her eyes. She nodded easily. "Very happy, brother."

"Good." He nodded once and laughed. "I hope the pregnancy hormones don't turn you into a fucking sap."

She let the tears fall graciously as she laughed. "Never, brother. I can still kick your ass."

Marcos smiled fondly, then in Spanish he said, "*Mamá estaría orgullosa de ti*" (Mom would be proud of you).

A small sob broke out of Kara, and Marcos hugged her to his chest.

"Shhh, lil *Manita*," Marcos murmured and stroked her back. "*Así como yo estoy orgulloso de ti, hermana. Eres lo mejor de nosotros y te mereces el mundo*" (just as I'm proud of you, sister. You're the best of us and deserve the world).

"I love you, brother," Kara spoke softly in English but loudly enough so her men could hear her so they would know she was alright.

Marcos pressed a kiss to her forehead and whispered another compliment in Spanish before he pulled away slowly. "I know you aren't burning my spaghetti sauce."

Kara laughed again and wiped at her eyes. "Sauce has been done for a while. I shut it off. We just need the noodles to boil."

"Already done, babe," Kevin spoke softly.

She looked up with red-rimmed eyes and met the eyes of her men. They each gave her a soft smile. "Did you start the garlic bread?" she asked.

"Just about finished." Derrick smirked. As if he'd summoned it, the timer on the oven dinged, indicating the bread was done.

Kara turned to the stovetop to see that the noodles were shut off and just waiting to be drained. "Well shit." She grinned. "Let's eat."

"Fuck yeah," Marcos agreed and headed for the table. "I'll just get out of your way."

The rest of the evening was comfortable and...fun. Kara was pleasantly surprised. Even when the talk had turned to club life, the boys had maintained a friendly banter. Marcos was candid about what was going on within his club and the bullshit his president was putting them all through while starting the war with the Ravager Knights that no one voted for.

"You need to figure out who's loyal to you," Johnny said, his voice gravelly at the end of the night.

They had moved out back to the firepit out past the pool. Kara was curled into an Adirondack chair, nursing a hot chocolate while she stared sleepily into the flames. The cool autumn night air pressed in around her, kept at bay a little longer by the roaring fire in front her. Someone had dropped a blanket around her shoulders, and she pulled it tighter as she curled into a ball.

Johnny and Marcos were to her right, but they spoke softly, letting the darkness settle around them and shape the seriousness of their conversation.

"I have a good idea. Several guys have approached me, bitchin' about Buckley," Marcos grumbled deeply. He took a sip of his beer and shook his head. "I don't have enough to overthrow him."

"What do you need?" Derrick shifted to Kara's left.

She looked away from the fire to see her big teddy bear looking sinister in the firelight. His thick beard and mane of hair were draped around his broad, heavily muscled shoulders, and his green eyes were almost glowing in the firelight.

Devil looked downright evil.

Her heart stuttered in her chest as he leaned forward and rested his elbows on his spread knees. "What do you need?" he asked again. It wasn't Derrick asking... Devil had come out to play.

Kara slowed her breathing, her lips parting as she stared at him. Her core clenched as her body heated with arousal. It was rare that she saw the Devil within Derrick.

Across the fire, Kevin was staring at her. His deep brown eyes were fixated on hers. She could feel the heat of his gaze on her while she stared at his brother with the same heat.

"I need Buckley to lose control so there's no doubt that he's no longer able to lead the club." Marcos growled, his fist clenching on the arm of the Adirondack chair. His knuckles cracked.

Kara looked away from Devil and turned toward her brother.

Marcos was always the calm before the storm, a stoic mask of indifference, but now he was a hairbreadth away from snapping. His clenching fists were the only visible signs that her brother was about to lose his cool. Had it been lighter outside, she'd probably be able to see the telltale ticking of his jaw, the vein that popped as he ground his molars with barely contained rage, a rage that he tried so hard to conceal around her.

She frowned slightly the longer she stared at her older brother. Ten years and a lifetime of memories, both together and apart, separated them. For all she was worried that she *didn't* know her brother, because he lied or omitted the truth when she was a child...at the end of day, she knew her brother's heart.

He wouldn't plan the murder of a man in front of her. He wouldn't unleash his absolute worst self in front of her. Not if he could help it.

Still feeling Kevin's burning gaze across the fire, she turned away from her brother and took in the dark-haired beauty in front of her. The firelight cast shadows and lit the sharp angles of Kevin's jaw and cheekbones. His eyes were onyx pools in the night, flames occasionally dancing in their reflections.

Kara's heart pounded in her chest as she met his smoldering gaze head-on. His lips were quirked ever so slightly in a smirk. Butterflies twisted in her belly as he continued to stare at her unblinkingly.

Heat colored her face as she stared at the man the club called Rockstar. The charming and cocky man before her was not her Kevin. He was Rockstar, the club's vice president. Charismatic and sinfully sexy.

His short black hair was styled into a short faux-hawk and glinted in the firelight as he tilted his head ever so slightly at Kara. His smirk deepened, as if he could read every damn dirty thought she had about him.

Unable to sit still any longer, the pulsing need between her legs growing in her awareness, Kara uncurled her legs and slowly stood up. Her legs tingled, half asleep, and she stumbled slightly as she stood.

Johnny's hand flew out and grabbed her elbow, steadying her and keeping her from falling into the fire. His blues eyes looked up at her with concern.

She smiled lazily. "I'm going to bed," she said softly.

He nodded and brushed his thumb over her arm.

Kara looked to his right as her brother slowly got to his feet. "Good night, Marquitos." She spoke softly and moved toward him.

He met her halfway and wrapped his arms around her. She felt how tense he was beneath her hands as she hugged him tightly. "I love you, big brother," she murmured.

"Back at you, lil *Manita*," he muttered.

She was immediately cold as she pulled away from her brother's safety and warmth. She needed to leave, though. Marcos would never get what he truly needed if he was worried about her.

She ignored her men and headed for the house, one hand clutching the fuzzy blanket wrapped around her shoulders, the other holding her empty hot chocolate mug. She walked through the sliding door off the kitchen and set her mug down on the counter.

She turned around to shut the sliding door and let out a quiet oomph as she slammed into an impenetrable wall of muscle. Her nose recognized the leather and mint scent of Kevin before her brain realized that he'd followed her into the house.

The door slid closed before large hands landed on her hips and encircled her waist. Her breath caught in her throat as he lifted her from the floor and set her on the granite counter. She held onto his shoulders, grasping at anything to keep her grounded.

Kevin pushed open her knees and stepped into her body. He pulled her to the edge of the counter so she was flush against him and claimed her mouth before she could speak. His kiss was dominating and sent butterflies fluttering in her belly as she sleepily tried to keep up.

She fucking loved it when he took control. "Kevin." She gasped and pulled away.

He kissed down her jaw and neck.

Kara reached for his belt and fumbled trying to open it. He laughed against her neck and assisted her, making quick work of dropping his pants. Then he pulled her off the counter, yanked her leggings down, and turned her around. He bent her over the kitchen counter and slammed into her without warning.

She screamed and tried to throw her head back in ecstasy only for his hand to fist in her hair and push her face down against the counter. "You have been driving me crazy all fucking night." He growled.

She smiled faintly as she panted. There was nothing for her to do but lay there and enjoy the ride. And what a ride it was. Kevin fucked her like a raging beast.

Her orgasm crashed over her, catching her by surprise. She moaned as tears welled in her eyes. Pleasure coated her nerves and sent sparks of ecstasy throughout her body. "Fuck," she mumbled, her legs weak.

"Such a good fucking doll." He moaned and fucked her harder if possible.

"Kevin, Kevin, oh fu—" She groaned loudly as another orgasm crashed into her.

"There's a good girl," he said, his voice raspy.

She was boneless. She floated on the counter, nothing but a limp bag of organs.

"You're so fucking perfect, baby. So perfect. I can't wait to see you grow with our baby. To see you grow round with our love," he rambled, panting slightly as he fucked her.

His words were dirty and sent shivers down her spine.

"Come for me again," he ordered.

"I can't," she said as she panted, though she could feel her body already on the verge again.

He reached around her and slid his fingers through her folds. He found her clit and pinched it between two fingers, tugging and toying with it until she was sobbing as she came again.

He followed her over the edge with a low groan before he stilled inside of her. He rested his head on her back, between her shoulder blades, as they both panted and caught their breath. "I love you, Kara," he said softly.

She smiled broadly and slowly pushed off the counter. He stood up and slowly slid out of her. She turned around and smiled up at him. "I love you, Kevin."

He gave her a panty-dropping smile before he leaned in and pressed a soft kiss to her mouth. "Let's get you to bed," he said against her lips before he helped her pull up her undies and leggings.

She winced at the feeling. She needed to clean up.

He tugged his jeans and belt back on quickly, then picked her up bridal style and headed upstairs.

She nuzzled into his neck and savored the moment.

Chapter Eleven

C HURCH WAS A SOMBER affair the Sunday afternoon following dinner with Marcos. Johnny had been stewing over it all day, and most of his guys had picked up on his mood when he'd grown short and angry. Johnny had called his club into church to discuss his meeting with Marcos Candela over the weekend. He wanted to be completely transparent. He didn't want to be accused of meeting the enemy in secret.

"As you all know, the three of us," Johnny motioned to himself, Kevin, and Derrick, "have taken Kara Carmichael as our old lady," he started, wanting to ease his guys into the backstory. "What many of you don't know is that Kara has an older brother with a different last name." Johnny paused and met several stares head-on. "Her brother is Marcos Candela, VP of the Devil's Psychos."

The reaction was immediate, as he thought it would be. His men were in an uproar and yelling their thoughts on the matter very clearly. To say they were upset was an understatement. Johnny leaned back in his chair and waited. Devil and Rockstar did the same on either side of him.

There was no point in yelling and arguing; his men needed the release. He'd be surprised if they didn't end up in the ring by the end of the night. The only other man not yelling and hollering was Lemmy.

Lemmy was an old-school biker who'd joined around the same time as Johnny's dad. He'd always been a powerhouse in the club and a voice of reason in church. He usually saw the bigger picture and didn't jump to conclusions. He was seventy, and at his age, he was lucky he was even able to ride anymore after the arthritis had started in on his hands. It wouldn't be long before he was forced to hang up his cut and retire from the club officially.

"What aren't you saying?" Lemmy asked, his voice hoarse from too many years smoking. He kept his voice low, not bothering to speak up over the hollering men.

They heard him, though. Lemmy was well respected within the club. When he spoke, people listened, brothers especially.

Johnny waited another moment as the room fell silent and their brothers looked between Johnny and Lemmy. Johnny nodded once to Lemmy and spoke. "As you know, Kara has been digging into my father's case and helping our club find justice for King's murder." Johnny had to clear his throat as emotions bore down on him. "Forty years ago, my father was in business with Vince Carmichael. They had been best friends in the Marines. Turns out they had dated the same girl—Carlita Candela—only they didn't know."

Hissing breaths echoed around the room as the reality of the situation settled on everyone—how their president had been betrayed by his best friend.

"Forty years ago, Carlita Candela got pregnant and told Mac the child was Vince's. Vince was already a hotshot lawyer, and she thought she'd have a better life with him than with a biker," Johnny explained. "Kara uncovered the paternity test from back in the day. Turns out Carlita lied to Mac, and the child was his. Marcos Candela is my half brother." He let the words hang in the room like a dead weight.

He watched as horror dawned on the faces of his brothers, his most trusted companions. His family. He watched the range of emotions cross over their faces.

Johnny met each man's eye as they slowly turned to study him in turn. While they were angry, and rightfully so, they also appeared resigned, as if they already knew what he was going to ask of them before he even asked it.

"What's this mean for the war against the Psychos?" Mammoth asked the million-dollar question. His heavy brow made him look like he was constantly scowling.

"That's why we're here." Johnny nodded and motioned around the room. "I had dinner with Marcos Saturday night," he explained. He was going for total honesty here.

Muttered curses went around the table as big, burly men shifted in their seats, uncomfortable.

"I called this meeting to be completely transparent with you, my brothers. Kara grew up not knowing her brother was a Psycho. He kept that from her all this time. She only found out a few weeks ago, and she didn't take the news well. They've had a rocky relationship in the last several months, and Kara invited him to dinner to try and mend the relationship," Johnny explained, running a hand over his buzzed blond hair. "They talked shit out, and they're good now. But it gave me an opportunity to talk to Marcos myself." He looked around the room slowly, meeting his brothers' stares.

"And what did the Psycho have to say for himself?" Welder asked, crossing his arms over his chest.

"He said Buckley's been acting on his own authority. He's been moving against his club and ours, without club votes. When his own guys question his moves, he shuts them down quick," Johnny said.

"He's gone full dictator." Devil spoke up for the first time. He turned to face the club. "Candela claims Buckley was the one to shoot Rachet in Alabama." Devil's hands clenched into fists on the tabletop, knuckles cracking.

"He also sent Nickle to spy on us without a club vote." Kevin interjected. He turned to his brothers and met their stares. "Buckley's brought in five new prospects without vetting them."

A hiss of muttered curses flew around the table as angry bikers growled in dissent. It was an unwritten biker law that any potential prospect had to be vetted and voted on accordingly. Most newcomers to the club were either family or friends or longtime coworkers. The club voted to let them prospect for the club. There was a process that Buckley had violated.

"Buckley's gone full dictator," Devil stated again.

"Marcos came to us and asked for help," Johnny stated clearly, once again meeting the stares around the table.

Men stilled in their chairs as silence settled over the room.

This was the true reason for their meeting: a vote. Johnny could not make this decision for the club himself. Each brother would have to decide whether or not they would be willing to aid the Devil's Psychos after the war between the two clubs had been initiated, after the deaths their family had already endured.

At the end of the day, the club was a democracy.

"I'm not asking you to vote tonight." Johnny kept his voice low, eyeing his men warily. "I'm asking you to consider the facts as we've presented them."

"How do we even know Marcos is telling the truth?" Welder grumbled.

Johnny ran a hand over his buzzed hair again. "You don't, not really." He shrugged. "I'm asking you to trust me, trust my judgment on this. Kara trusts her brother. I'm trusting her and, by extension, Marcos." Johnny spoke frankly, leaving no misconceptions on the table.

"I told Marcos to find out who's loyal to him and who's loyal to Buckley. We'll have a sit-down with Marcos later this week, see if we can broker some kind of...deal," Johnny hedged.

There was a murmuring of agreement around the table.

Johnny banged the gavel on the table and dismissed the session of church. Guys were quick to stand from their seats and leave the room. He couldn't blame them. He had laid a heavy truth on them. They would have a lot to digest and think over.

Anxious and angry, they would spend the rest of the night drinking to numb their minds.

·

It was late when Johnny and Kevin were able to leave the clubhouse. Derrick had checked out earlier, not wanting to leave their girl home alone, but Johnny and Kevin hadn't been able to leave. They had to be available to their brothers who had questions. After the church session, they had needed time to come to terms with what Johnny was asking. It was asking a lot.

By the time Johnny and Kevin pulled into the garage of the house, it was after one a.m. The house was dark, as was to be expected. Kara was so tired most of the time she had started taking naps in the afternoon. She had been grateful Taylor Construction had finished her office at the Carmichael building while she'd been out with her injuries. Now she could nap on her couch in peace without someone seeing her through what had once been glass walls.

Johnny and Kevin made quick work of taking off their boots by the back door in the mudroom before they headed through the kitchen. Johnny grabbed two bottles of water out of the fridge and tossed one to Kevin, who caught it on the fly.

They padded upstairs on silent feet, each hoping to be the one to slide into bed next to their girl and not get stuck next to Derrick for the night. Even with the bigger bed, they'd rather sleep next to their girl than their bro.

The sight that greeted them was not of a peaceful, restful nature. Turns out they hadn't had to mind their steps as they'd slinked through the dark house or worry about who would be sliding in next to her.

Because Kara was awake…and she was riding Derrick's cock.

Her head was thrown back, one of her hands fisted into her long blond hair. It trailed down her naked back, swaying between the dimples of her lower back. Smooth creamy skin glistened in the faint moonlight shining in from the open windows.

Her hips swiveled and rose slowly as she chased her own high. Soft breathy moans filled the air. Derrick's large hands were a stark contrast on her narrow waist, his fingers gripping her soft flesh as he guided her hips over his.

Johnny and Kevin stood frozen in the doorway, both men mesmerized by their girl. Kara's free hand came up and twisted into her blond mane along with the first, both hands clenching her hair, as if she were imagining it was one of them.

"There's a good girl," Johnny crooned from his spot in the doorjamb.

Kara didn't startle; she barely tilted her head in acknowledgement—she was close. Johnny could tell by her breathing, by the way Derrick's fingers tightened on her waist. Her breaths came out in short little gasps, and her back arched further.

Kevin moved across the room and knelt on the bed beside Kara. He fisted his hand into her hair beside both of hers. He was rough as he tilted her head back and claimed her mouth in a filthy kiss. Johnny couldn't help but be thoroughly turned on as he watched his brother's mouth slide against Kara's, their lips opening and tongues battling.

She let out breathy little moans of pleasure as he fucked her mouth with his tongue.

Johnny couldn't take it any longer. He walked across the room and joined Kevin on the mattress. He slid his hands up the bare skin of Kara's back and around her chest until he was cupping her heavy breasts in both hands. He leaned forward and sucked a kiss into her neck while she made out with Kevin. "Come for me, Princess," he ordered, his voice gravelly in her ear as his fingers pinched her nipples.

Her breathing shuddered, and her body began to shake. One of Derrick's hands left her waist and slid down to her folds. His thumb circled her clit, and her whole body arched and seized as the orgasm rolled over her. "Such a good girl," Johnny crooned again, rolling her nipples between his fingers.

Her body went limp, and she would have fallen forward if it hadn't been for the three of them holding her up.

Kevin broke the kiss as Kara panted to catch her breath.

"Why are you awake, pretty Momma?" Johnny asked softly before he pressed a kiss to her sweaty temple.

"You weren't home. Couldn't sleep," she mumbled, her voice throaty.

Johnny's heart squeezed in his chest. He hated that she missed him, hated that he had to be away from her. "We're home now, Princess." He nodded before he claimed her mouth in a soft and sensual kiss.

"What should we do to help you sleep?" Kevin asked, his voice low as he rubbed her shoulders.

"Fuck me," she mumbled, still half asleep.

"Oh, we'll fuck you alright," Johnny promised. He grabbed her hips and lifted her off Derrick's cock. He turned her around, reverse cowgirl, and guided her back down on Derrick's still-hard dick. Devil's hands came up and helped her mount him.

Then Johnny pushed her backward, so her back was flush with Derrick's chest. His hands slid up her sides and cupped her breasts.

Johnny and Kevin slowly got naked, their eyes never leaving the pair on the bed, watching as Derrick's cock slid in and out of her glistening cunt. Even in the dim light, Johnny could see how wet she was, how she dripped down Devil's cock.

He wouldn't even need lube for what he was about to do. He grabbed it anyway and coated his cock liberally. "You ready for this, Princess?" he asked roughly.

"Mmm," she hummed.

He smirked. She would be waking up shortly. He glanced at Derrick and waited. Devil nodded back and Johnny knelt on the bed. He slid up between their open legs and rubbed his fingers over Kara's clit.

"Oh," she moaned low. Her eyes were shut, and her head listed sideways. She was barely conscious.

"You want me to fuck you?" Johnny asked her.

"Always," she murmured, a slow smile pulling across her luscious lips.

Johnny grabbed the head of his cock and guided it to her hole. He pressed his cock to her cunt beside Derrick's, and Kara groaned deeply.

"Relax baby girl," Derrick said, and he slid his hands around her hips. One hand found her clit and rubbed slowly; the other reached for a nipple and pinched roughly.

Kara moaned, and Johnny was able to pop the head of his cock inside her. He slid in slowly, groaning as he bottomed out.

"So fucking perfect," Kevin said as he knelt on the bed next to Kara's face.

"I'm not gonna last. Fuck," Derrick groaned.

Johnny smirked. "My dick feel that good rubbing against yours?" he shot at him.

"Fuck yeah, it does." Derrick groaned.

Kara giggled softly.

"Open up," Kevin instructed.

Kara complied immediately, and Kevin slid his dick in her mouth. Her lips closed around his head, her hand coming up and wrapping around the base of his cock, pumping him slowly. He moaned and closed his eyes. "Fucking love your mouth, baby," he muttered, mostly to himself.

Johnny twisted his hips, and both Kara and Derrick groaned. "That's right." Johnny smirked. "Who's going to be good and come for me?" he asked.

"Fuck you, dude," Devil grumbled.

"Fucking you both right now." He laughed.

Kara's breathing picked up as she started panting. She pulled off Kevin's cock. "Don't stop." She whimpered before Kevin grabbed her jaw and guided her back to his dick.

"Never Princess," Johnny vowed.

Derrick thrust up into her. They found a pace, and soon Kara was a moaning, whining mess between them. She whimpered and writhed on top of Derrick. "Oh fuck," Kevin groaned, his hips stuttering and slowing.

Kara moaned loudly and shook as her walls clamped down on Johnny's and Devil's cocks. Her pussy gushed as she came hard enough to squirt.

"Fuck!" Derrick groaned as he found his own release.

Johnny picked up the pace and fucked into her harder. He only needed a few more pumps before he followed everyone over the edge into fucking bliss.

Fucking hell, there was nothing better in the world than fucking his girl.

Chapter Twelve

"**B**ABY GIRL, HOW ARE we supposed to know what to buy if you don't know what you're having?" Derrick asked from across the clothing section of the baby department store.

Kara smiled. "We're here for furniture. We're just getting distracted," she answered as she sorted through a rack of green and yellow infant sleepers.

"It's all so fucking small." Kevin sighed and held up a blue and gray onesie pack.

Kara grinned at him. She never would have imagined her three rough and tumble men would be down for a shopping trip, but when Johnny had suggested it that morning, she'd jumped at the chance. It had only been a week, but her boys had already moved things out of the bedroom next to theirs and were talking about knocking down the wall that weekend.

"Is this a good idea?" Derrick asked, frowning. He was holding up another set of baby clothes and looked upset.

"What's wrong?" Kara asked when she took in his disheartened expression.

Derrick shook himself out of it and put down the clothes he was holding. He looked up, and his green eyes met hers. She could visibly see him trying to force back emotions and put on a bright smile for her.

She saw through his bullshit, though. "Derrick." She sighed and put down the baby clothes she had been holding. "Talk to me," she murmured and moved through the racks closer to him. Out of the corner of her eye, she saw Johnny and Kevin drift away to give them privacy. She slid her hands around his waist and leaned in to him.

He sighed and wrapped his arms around her waist, pulling her against him.

She rested her head against his chest and closed her eyes. She breathed in his scent and warmth and waited for him to speak his mind. She didn't push him; she knew him well enough to know that he would say what he was thinking.

"I was just talking to my sister, and she mentioned that generally most women don't tell anyone until after the twelfth week 'cause if something happened...and shopping before then could be considered bad luck."

Kara stiffened and then forced herself to relax. "Yes, many women wait until after the first trimester is over. It is generally considered that there's less chance of a miscarriage after twelve weeks. But that's not something I can control. I'm young and healthy. My doctor said there's no reason to worry. It's out of our hands anyway, if something were to happen. So why not enjoy all nine months of it instead of worrying for the first trimester?"

Derrick sighed, but some of the tension in his body dissipated.

"I'm past most of the sickness too. I'm eight weeks pregnant as of tomorrow. My appointment is tomorrow. You can come and ask the doctor all the questions you want, OK?" she reasoned, trying to put his mind and concerns at ease.

"I'm scared," he admitted softly, squeezing her tighter.

She pulled away just enough to look up at him. His emerald eyes were staring down at her; she could see the emotion swimming in their depths. "I am too," she admitted. "This wasn't on the radar anytime soon for me."

"I never thought I wanted kids..." He rubbed a hand over his beard. "But the moment you were sick and Johnny told us what was going on...I'd never been so happy," he murmured. Tears lined his eyes, and he squeezed her tighter. "The thought of losing the baby never crossed my mind."

Kara squeezed Derrick back just as hard as he was squeezing her. "I feel the same way. It's scary and anything can happen, but the risks aren't high. Anything can happen to anyone every single day. We can't live in fear of the unknown." She gave him a bright smile, pushed up onto her tippy-toes, and pressed a kiss to his lips.

He slid his hand up her side and cupped the back of her neck. His fingers dug in as he held her to him and poured his love and fear into that kiss. She closed her eyes and moaned, opening her mouth to meet his passion.

She was breathless when he broke the kiss a while later. Her eyes fluttered open and she looked up at him. The mischievous sparkle had returned to his emerald orbs. "Better?" she asked him.

He gave her a soft smile. "Great," he answered, grinding his rock-hard cock against her.

She smirked and pulled away. "Let's pick out furniture and get out of here."

"Yes, Momma," Derrick drawled.

Kara shot him a look as she walked away, heading in search of Johnny and Kevin. "No," she said over her shoulder.

"Baby girl, you don't tell me no." Derrick smirked and stalked toward her.

"Don't use *Momma* in a sexual way then," she shot back at him.

"No mommy kink. Got it." Derrick chuckled as he came to stand before her again.

Kara rolled her eyes but gave him a kiss on the corner of his mouth. "Let's go pick a crib and dresser set."

Derrick nodded and held her hand as they headed toward the furniture section.

Tuesday's appointment came faster than Kara thought possible. She left the Carmichael building around four and headed over to the doctor's office with her boys following behind her on their bikes. They were dying to come with her and ask the doctor a million questions. She only hoped they would behave in the office and not act like fools.

The nurse had given them a funny look when Kara told her the three men would be coming back with her. Thankfully it was a smaller practice, so there weren't too many people in the waiting room.

"Alright Miss Kara," Rori, the pretty brunette nurse, said with smile. "Let's get your weight and blood pressure." She motioned toward the scale first.

Kara kicked off her black heels and stepped onto the scale in just her stocking feet. Her men fanned out in the room around her, making her smile. Johnny stayed near the door in case of an intruder; it was always safety first with him.

Rori caught her smile and chuckled. "They always like that?" She nodded at the men.

Kara smiled and nodded. "Most of the time," she answered, speaking as if they weren't in the room.

"Is this a who's-the-daddy situation?" Rori asked with a non-judgmental grin on her face.

"It's none of your business," Johnny snapped gruffly.

"We're raising 'em together," Derrick shot out.

Kara laughed and shook her head. "It's more of a why-choose situation." She grinned, stressing the *why choose* part.

"Aah." Understanding dawned on Rori's face. Her chocolate eyes lit up. "Lucky girl."

"Sure am." Kara nodded and glanced over her shoulder at her boys. They all beamed back at her with pride, even Johnny's grumpy ass.

"My sister's been with four guys for the last five years or so. They have three kids together. They make it work," Rori said with a laugh. She wrote down Kara's weight and motioned to the chair.

"Four? Damn." Kara huffed out a breath as she slipped back into her heels and headed for the chair next to the counter. "I barely can keep up with three." She laughed as she took a seat and put her arm on the counter.

"Right? My sister calls them her harem." Rori laughed.

Kara giggled and glanced at her men. They smiled and rolled their eyes at her.

"More power to you ladies, though. Lots to be jealous of over here," Rori said with a grin. She placed a blood pressure cuff around Kara's bicep and slid her stethoscope into her ears while placing the end near Kara's inner elbow.

Kara spent the next several minutes answering medical questions: the date of her last period and other stuff. They spent several minutes going over family medical histories. She was extremely grateful the boys had decided to come after all. She would have had no idea how to answer several of the questions. Apparently she didn't know her men as well as she'd thought.

The idea left her feeling unsettled. They really hadn't been dating long, going on almost four months, and somehow, she was pregnant and living with them already. She didn't know why the thought bothered her.

"Alright, let's get you across the hall to ultrasound, and we'll set you up with Aeyla. She'll show you a picture of your little peanut." Rori smiled brightly.

They followed Rori across the hall and into the ultrasound room, where they found a young black woman with light skin and a mass of light brown curls pulled back from her face with a large headband. She had the largest and lightest blue eyes Kara had ever seen. She was a gorgeous woman, and she had a wide, toothy grin for Kara and her boys as they walked in.

"Alright Miss Aeyla, this is Kara and her harem of men." Rori grinned and waved at the men.

Kara laughed while her guys rolled their eyes.

"A reverse harem! I love it!" Aeyla grinned. "Come on in and have a seat." She motioned toward the medical chair in the center of the room next to a large computer monitor. "I'm Aeyla," she introduced herself, pronouncing her name like Kayla but minus the K. "Mom, you take the chair here in the center. Daddies can fight over the other chair and stand behind you. You should all be able to see the monitor that way."

Kara took her seat and laughed, instantly liking the girl.

Aeyla took a seat on a wheeled stool and rolled right up next to Kara and the machines. "Alright girlie, you are about eight weeks exactly, according to the date of your last period. So let's take a look and see if the fetus size matches that and say hi to your little nugget," Aeyla said in a smooth, almost singsongy way as she looked over Kara's chart.

Kara smiled and immediately felt at ease.

"Alright, I'm gonna need you to lift up your shirt and we'll take a look," Aeyla directed.

Kara lifted her shirt enough to expose her belly.

"Alrighty, this should be warm." Aeyla squirted gel from a bottle on Kara's belly.

Kara nodded and then Aeyla got to work. She moved the ultrasound wand over her belly, pressing down as she watched the screen.

Instantly her boys moved in closer around her. Kevin slid into the chair next to her and laced their fingers together. She looked over at him with a smile; his eyes were glued to the screen.

Derrick pressed in against Kevin's back. He leaned over the chair and Kevin's shoulder and placed his hand on Kara's shoulder. He gave her a gentle squeeze and left his hand there.

Johnny pressed against the back of the medical chair on Kara's other side. He was squeezed next to the chair and the computer, his eyes never leaving the screen.

"Aah, here we go." Aeyla grinned and stopped moving the wand. On the screen there was a small, round blob-looking thing. "That looks exactly like an eight-week fetus." Aeyla grinned. "Congratulations parents!"

Hands squeezed her body as her guys held onto her. Tears welled in her eyes as she looked from her little blob of a baby on the screen to each of her men and saw the tears lining their eyes as well. This was really happening. They were happy and in love, and they were going to be parents.

Kara committed the moment to memory. She would never forget the looks on her men's faces; it was one of the happiest moments of her life.

Chapter Thirteen

FRIDAY NIGHT IN THE clubhouse usually meant a party. Usually Marcos would have a couple shots, sip a beer, and enjoy the chick sitting on his lap while surrounded by his brothers.

That was before things had gone to shit, before Buckley had divided their club and started a war with the fucking Ravager Knights.

Now, the party still raged, but it was more subdued. There was an uneasy air around the room. Brothers met the eyes of other brothers and wondered if they were still loyal to each other or to Buckley. Stone and Dagger were seated next to Marcos, nursing their beers. The only thing missing was a chick perched on Marcos's knee, but in this climate...he was not in the mood.

"Have you talked to anyone?" Marcos asked Stone softly while looking around to see who was watching or listening.

"My dad and Bear are on the fence," Stone admitted, shifting in the chair next to Marcos.

Marcos nodded slowly, rubbing his jaw. He could see that; they were from the older generation. They had prospected with Buckley back in the day. They would have to be convinced of a better way. Things would have to be lined up first before they would jump ship.

"Axel, Blaze, and Phoenix want to meet away from the clubhouse. I think they'll be on board." Nico nodded.

"Trick and Ransom are down. So is Nickle," Marcos said.

"I'll get my dad and Bear to come meet when we meet up with Axel, Blaze, and Phoenix," Stone said.

"And Ace?" Nico asked.

"Ace is so far up Buckley's ass," Marcos growled. "Leave him out of it. Prospects too."

Ace was another longtime member from the same generation as Bear, Jerry, and Buckley. He was a hothead on a good day and a downright psycho on a bad day. There was no telling what the asshole would do. He was a loose cannon.

Marcos hated the guy. With his beady black eyes and bald head, he was a fucking short little fat dude with no neck and massive arms that made him look like a gorilla. He kissed Buckley's ass and was generally a dick to everyone else.

"Agreed," Nico muttered.

There was a commotion in the corner of the room where Buckley was usually holed up with Ace. Like clockwork tonight, Buckley and Ace were at their round table with the prospects surrounding them. They had been snorting coke all night.

Marcos looked over just as Ace stood from the table, shouting at Buckley.

The girls that had been serving them whisky all night had slowly started to back away from the table as Buckley started shouting back. One thing the girls learned early here was to stay out of club drama.

Buckley stood up just as quickly and was reaching for his nine before anyone could stop him.

"Oh shit!" Marcos yelled and dove for cover as Buckley started shooting.

Marcos, Stone, and Nico managed to dive behind a pool table as the shots rang out. Buckley fired until Ace fell back, then he turned his gun on the prospect in front of him.

When the sound of the hammer hitting the empty gun rang out across the room, Marcos stood slowly. Nico and Stone were on either side of him, unharmed.

He couldn't say the same for Ace or the prospect.

"Shit, Janey," someone muttered.

One of the women that had been serving Buckley's crew had been caught in the cross fire. Even from across the room, Marcos could see the blond was dead, along with the prospect—and Ace.

Buckley killed a patched brother.

"You dumb fuck," Bear growled.

Buckley was still staring down at Ace with the anger and rage on his face. He was so coked out of his mind he didn't even hear Bear.

Marcos took the opportunity as VP to make a move. "Grab him," he ordered Trick and Ransom, who had been sitting at the bar just to the right of the shooting.

Buckley didn't fight as the gun was pried from his hand. Trick and Ransom made quick work of patting him down for additional weapons.

Bear and Jerry moved in and helped Trick and Ransom escort Buckley to the basement cells that they used for interrogations.

"You four," Marcos motioned at the four remaining prospects, "church," Marcos ordered.

For a moment the four men, stringy and lanky, looked like they were going to run or reach for weapons. Stone and Dagger moved toward them. "Lose the weapons," Stone ordered.

Marcos spared a glance at the dead bodies on the ground. Janey's dirty blond hair, splattered with blond, made Marcos pause. Made him think of another woman with dirty blond hair, splattered with blood the last time he saw her, before she left him.

He shook himself from his reverie and glanced at who was still in the room. Axel, Blaze, and Phoenix moved in so Marcos could see them. "Clear the room. We'll deal with the bodies after we deal with the prospects," Marcos ordered.

"We're in unprecedented times for this club," Marcos started as he sat at the head of the table in church. His club was fanned out around the table. For the moment he was allowing the four remaining prospects to sit in; he'd deal with them in a bit.

"Our club has been fracturing around us for the last several months," Marcos continued. He looked around the table, meeting the stares of every man that dared to meet his and noting those that kept their gazes glued on the table. "We have a problem: our president has forgotten the rules of this brotherhood."

Murmurs of agreement rippled around the table.

"First matter of business, though." Marcos turned toward the four prospects at the end of the table. None of the men would return his gaze. One fidgeted in his seat. "With Buckley's presidency under scrutiny, I motion to kick the prospects until we can vet them properly."

"Seconded," Stone replied immediately.

The prospects froze in their seats, the largest of the four of them finally meeting Marcos's gaze. There was a look of contempt in his dark eyes, but Marcos didn't give a shit. He wanted the scum gone.

"Buckley promised us the patch," he said.

Marcos glared at the scrawny fucker. "Buckley's in hot shit with his club. You ain't part of this club. Take off the cut and leave."

Another ripple of murmurings circled the table. For once it seemed the club was on the same page.

A moment later, the four prospects stood with a scuffing of their chairs. "Buckley was right about you," their pseudo leader shot at Marcos with contempt.

Marcos glared through a smirk. "I could give a shit what you've got to say, bro."

"That's not what your sister said." He smirked.

"The fuck you say?" Marcos shouted. He shot out of his chair and lunged for the shit-talking dead man.

Dagger reached the fucker first and slammed him face-first on the table.

Marcos pushed his friend away and grabbed the prospect by the collar of his shirt before he reared back and landed a punch to the asshole's face.

Blood rushed in his ears, and his vision narrowed to the asshole he started to punch over and over. Someone was yelling; hands grabbed at him. He fought them all off as he continued to beat the prospect's face.

"Marc!" Stone shouted in his ear.

Someone bear-hugged him from behind and physically lifted him off the prospect. He was tossed back against the doors leading into church. Dagger got in his face. "He got the message, brother."

Marcos panted as he caught his breath and let his temper simmer down. The motherfucking prospect was a bloody mess, sprawled out on the table. His chest rose and fell, but he was otherwise unconscious. Marcos cursed in Spanish and walked back to his seat at the head of the table.

Dagger and Stone hauled the prospect off the table and shoved him at the other three. "Take that with you," Stone snapped.

Marcos sat heavily at the head of the table and met the stares of his brothers as they settled back in their seats. "We vote on the prospects," Marcos said, not wasting any time.

"Aye." The group voted almost immediately and unanimously.

Marcos nodded and slammed the gavel down. "Next course of business: Buckley."

"He killed a patched brother," Stone ground out.

"He's been erratic for a while now. Coke's been out of hand," Bear rumbled across the table.

Marcos nodded once at his brother. He appreciated the old-timer's speaking up against the latest indiscretions.

"He pulled us into a war with the Ravager Knights without a vote," Axel added.

Marcos leveled a stare at Axel. He wasn't close with the man. Axel, Blaze, and Phoenix were their own tight unit, kinda like Stone, Dagger, and Marcos. The two groups didn't hang out much at all, outside club shit.

Marcos nodded once. "I've spoken to most of you lately about my feelings on the club and Buckley as president." He motioned around the room. "Axel, Blaze, Phoenix, we haven't had a chance to speak yet, but I'm changing that now. Too much has gone down tonight, and recently with Nickle," he nodded at the man, "to ignore. Buckley is not acting in the best interest of this club. He has been using this club as his personal army to fight a war that shouldn't be club business, period."

"What do you mean?" Axel spoke up, his low voice rough and gravelly. His dark eyes narrowed under the baseball hat he wore.

"Buckley has been working with Vince Carmichael, of Carmichael and Associates, on a forty-year vendetta against King Taylor. Back in the day, they both loved the same woman. Turns out the woman was my mother," Marcos explained.

"Holy shit," Bear and Jerry muttered.

Axel, Blaze, and Phoenix looked on with stony faces. Trick and Ransom observed in disbelief.

"What the fuck?" Nickle asked.

Marcos nodded. "For those of you that don't know, my sister Kara has been helping the Ravager Knights with Mac Taylor's case against Vince Carmichael, her father."

"Holy shit," Blaze whispered in awe.

Marcos nodded and continued. "Yeah, she's been digging through years of files from her father's law firm and came across a paternity test from forty years ago. Turns out my father was Mac Taylor." Marcos sighed and looked around the room. Shocked and dismayed faces returned his gaze.

"Holy shit," Bear grumbled.

Marcos only nodded, his eyes on Axel, Blaze, and Phoenix. Those three would end up casting the deciding votes. Right now, though, he couldn't get a read on the three of them. Blaze was looking more than a little stunned.

"Vince Carmichael has been meeting with Buckley monthly. You've probably seen him around over the years. Most of us called him the suit," Marcos explained.

"Fuck," Phoenix cursed.

"So the suit has been using our club to get revenge on your old man?" Axel asked, laying out everything in layman's terms.

"Well, yeah, basically. If you want to simplify it like that, Buckley has started a war against the Knights on behalf of Vince Carmichael. He's even struck a deal with Las Serpientes."

"Motherfucker," Axel growled, anger radiating off his form.

Marcos briefly remembered Axel's having a younger brother who was killed by Las Serpientes when the two of them had still been in high school. It was part of the reason that Axel had joined up to begin with.

"You know this for sure?" Jerry Langford, Stone's father, asked.

"I heard them myself." Marcos sighed, meeting his gaze.

"Fucking hell." Jerry sighed and ran a hand over his buzzed gray hair.

"My sister is dating Mayhem, Rockstar, and Devil," Marcos also added, feeling the need for total transparency.

Axel raised an eyebrow at that. "You're OK with that?" Marcos vaguely remembered Axel, Phoenix, and Blaze dating a girl together for a while.

Marcos rubbed a hand over his skull trimmed hair. "I'm coming around to it," he admitted. "Mostly because she's my baby sister."

"And he's your half brother?" Axel shot back, raising an eyebrow.

Marcos chuckled and shook his head. "I'm still coming around on that one too," he admitted.

"So what are you asking us, son?" Bear asked, bringing the conversation back to business.

Marcos met his gaze. "I'm asking this club to consider a truce with the Ravager Knights. We hand over Buckley to Mayhem, let them dish out the justice they deserve for the deaths of King Taylor and Rachet, and end the war Buckley started without a vote."

A heavy silence rang out around the room as the men froze in their chairs to digest Marcos's proposal. As the silence continued, Marcos shifted in his chair and looked around.

Heavy stares met his gaze. It was a hard choice. A brotherhood was fractured, their president had betrayed them. These were unprecedented times for their club. The Devil's Psychos had never gone through an upheaval as great as this one before, and their brotherhood was shaken to its core.

"A truce?" Blaze asked, his voice low.

"Yes." Marcos nodded. "No more war. Let it all go."

"And you're OK with that?" Blaze asked Nickle, who sat across the table from him.

Nickle nodded. "I am actually. Buckley forced me to spy on the Knights that night, said he'd kill my old lady if I didn't do what he said."

Hisses of rage rippled around the table.

"The Knights, by rights, should have killed me for spying on them. It's nothing short of what any of us would have done," Nickle explained. "They showed mercy, let me live."

"Fucking hell," Jerry muttered, shaking his head.

"Buckley's been unstable for too long. He's been acting like a dictator for too long," Stone said.

"Agreed." Marcos nodded.

"I want to hear it from him," Bear said.

Marcos nodded and shrugged a shoulder. "Let's go ask him."

It only took a few minutes for them to exit church and head down the basement stairs to the holding cells. The unfinished basement housed a couple of holding cells, with drains set into the concrete floor. Buckley was sprawled out unconscious on the floor in the center of his cell.

Dagger immediately grabbed the hose in the corner and sprayed cold water on Buckley's face. The weathered man sputtered, gasping for breath because he wasn't wearing his oxygen. His white hair shone brightly in the florescent lights in the basement, emphasizing his age.

Marcos didn't give a damn, though. This man had torn apart his club over a personal vendetta. He had betrayed the brotherhood, killed a patched member without reason. He was the scum of the earth and deserved to be put down. And Marcos would be glad to do it.

Marcos unlocked the cell and stepped inside.

Buckley's gray eyes were maniacal in their rage as he glared up at Marcos. "You fucking bastard." Buckley spat.

Marcos cursed in Spanish. "You're pathetic," he said in English.

"What deal do you have with Vince Carmichael?" Bear broke in as he stepped into the holding cell. He crossed his beefy arms over his chest and waited.

Marcos loomed over Buckley, also waiting.

Buckley gasped for breath, a smug smirk spreading across his lips. "I hear the Ravager Knights have been ravaging your sister's sweet pussy."

Marcos let out a roar of rage as he lunged for the bastard who was still lying on the ground. He managed to get in several kicks before he was pulled off Buckley.

Buckley was left rolling and groaning in pain.

Marcos stalked away, huffing with anger. He needed to get his shit under control. He couldn't kill the man, not if he wanted a truce with the Ravager Knights. He needed the war to end, and quickly. He couldn't have his sister living with them if there was any kind of tension between the two clubs.

Stone moved into the cell and got in Buckley's face. "What's the deal with Carmichael?"

Buckley gasped for breath and let out a hoarse laugh. "Like you aren't going to kill me once I tell you the truth?"

"I'm going to rip you apart, limb by limb," Marcos growled.

"Did you threaten Nickle's old lady?" Bear asked.

Buckley laughed. "That slut's been begging for my cock for months."

"The fuck she has!" Nickle snapped. He stormed into the cell and barely got his own kick in before Bear was hauling him back.

"You killed a brother without a vote, you started a war without a vote. You went behind the club's back and worked with our enemy Las Serpientes. What do you have to say for yourself?" Bear asked, his voice a deep rumble.

"I did it all," Buckley rasped and let out a choked laugh. "I'd do it all again. This club has turned into a bunch of pussies."

"You're a disgrace. You've disgraced the patch and this club," Bear said. He spat on the ground next to Buckley.

Buckley just laughed.

Jerry shook his head. "He's too coked out."

"Doesn't matter. He confessed," Marcos pressed. "We vote now."

"Aye," came instantly from Stone, Dagger, and Nickle.

Marcos looked at Jerry. "Aye," he said, shaking his head in disgust.

Trick and Ransom moved closer. "Aye," they both said with a nod to Marcos.

Marcos turned to Axel, Blaze, and Phoenix. All three men looked down at Buckley with contempt and disgust. "Aye," they voted one after the other.

"Aye," Marcos voted last. "I'll set it up."

Chapter Fourteen

"**C**ome on Carmichael! You've gotta give me something here." Freddy Danvers griped as he paced through Johnny's great room.

Kara rolled her eyes and sipped her lemonade from her perch on a barstool at the kitchen island. She glanced at the woman sitting across from her.

District Attorney Lacey Winters was dressed as casually as Kara had ever seen her. Her auburn hair was down in soft waves around her shoulders. Her cashmere sweater was a soft gray color and paired with black leggings that made her look downright comfortable. Her sharp hazel eyes missed nothing though.

She sipped her whisky and tilted her head at Kara. "I'm not saying you haven't been cooperative," she started.

Kara leveled a stare at the DA and raised an eyebrow.

"I'm not," she said, immediately raising her hands in surrender. "You have literally handed over everything and *then some*," Lacey admitted. "I'm just hoping you have a little bit more up your sleeve. We're at a loss at this point."

They might not have been friends before this adventure, but they had run in the same circles and were always friendly. Colleagues. Kara could easily see that changing. The woman was a hard-ass, and Kara respected her for it.

Kara sighed. "I honestly have no idea. We know he has an office offshore. I'm having Jack Adams dig further into Carlita Associates and any properties my father might own down there. I need an address."

"Who is this Jack Adams?" Lacey asked, eyebrows furrowing.

"He's *the* Jack Adams," Danvers said immediately, almost reverently. "He's a tech genius and the CEO of Adams Inc. He's a fucking *genius*."

Kara nodded and flicked her hand at Danvers. "What he said, but he's Kevin's brother."

"I won't be able to push for extradition." Lacey frowned. "Not for white-collar crimes."

"I'm not worried about extradition," Kara said evenly, shaking her head slowly.

Lacey stared at her head-on. "I can't be involved in anything il—"

"Don't worry about it." Kara shook her head again. "You worry about winning your case. I'll worry about getting him on US soil."

Danvers grinned wickedly. "You've got an army at your disposal."

Kara rolled her eyes at the criminal lawyer, a smirk on her lips. "How is it that you're so brilliant but such an idiot too?"

"You know, Carmichael. One of these days, you'll leave these men of yours for me." Danvers smirked.

"I'm in with these men for at least the next eighteen years, so you'll be waiting awhile," Kara snarked back.

Lacey's lips parted slightly in shock before she glanced down at Kara's plain lemonade. She laughed. "Congratulations."

"Thanks." Kara smiled easily at the DA. She had a likable quality to her.

"Well shit," Danvers swore.

Kara rolled her eyes but was saved from having to knock him down a peg by the opening of the back door in the kitchen. Kara looked over just as all three of her guys came filing in. It was just past eight on a Friday night, early for them, but she watched them all take in the scene in the kitchen warily.

"Hey guys," Kara greeted with a smile.

"Hey babe," Kevin murmured as he walked over and wrapped his arms around Kara from behind.

"Hi." She smiled and looked up at him over her shoulder.

He pressed a kiss to the crown of her head.

"What's going on here?" Johnny asked, stepping into the kitchen.

"Danvers." Derrick nodded. He headed for the fridge. "Winters," he added as an afterthought.

Lacey smirked at Kara. "Freddy boy and I came over to chat with Kara, see if she had any leads on where her father might be."

Johnny's eyes narrowed on the DA and Danvers. He stalked around the island until he was standing beside Kara. "She's already given you everything she has." He practically growled at the district attorney.

Kara reached out and slid her hand down Johnny's inked forearm until she laced their fingers together. "They know that," Kara told him. "We just need to find my father and Laraway."

"My brother is working on that," Kevin said, frowning.

"I know." Kara sighed. "Once he does find them, we need to bring them in quickly. Which, of course, we all know *already*," Kara stressed and turned to Danvers. "Danvers was just saying how he was leaving." She tilted her head at him and smiled.

Kevin's arms squeezed her tighter and pulled her back against his chest.

Kara held Johnny's hand as she leaned against Kevin. She gave Danvers a knowing smirk, and the older man rolled his eyes. "Alright, alright, I'm leaving," Danvers said good-naturedly.

"Me too." Lacey sighed. "Let me know if you find anything, Kara."

Kara nodded. "You know I will."

"I know. I appreciate everything you've already done. I really don't mean to make it seem like you haven't been cooperative—"

"'Cause I handed that case over to you on a silver fucking platter." Kara smiled wryly. "Like I said, you worry about building and winning this case. I'll worry about getting you my father and Laraway."

"Hard to win a case without a defendant," Danvers shot out, looking smug.

Kara rolled her eyes again, but Derrick was the one to move away from the fridge and head toward Danvers. "Thought you were leaving?" he asked, moving in closer.

When they were almost chest to chest, Danvers smirked and nodded. "Right. Always a great time working with the Ravager Knights," he said before he tipped his head at Derrick and headed for the front door.

Derrick rolled his eyes when the front door shut and walked back around the island to Kara. He squeezed in on Kara's left side and pressed a kiss to her temple. "We'll remind him who pays his checks tomorrow," Derrick promised.

Kara laughed. "I'm not worried about Danvers. He's an idiot, but he's right. We need to find my father ASAP." Kara sighed.

"We will," Kevin said, squeezing her against him again.

"Alright, let me know when you know something," Lacey said and stood up from her barstool. "You guys have a good night."

A chorus of *good nights* followed her out of the house.

Once she was gone, Kara sighed and closed her eyes.

Kevin turned with her in her arms. Johnny let go of her hand and then pressed against her front, tilting her head back as he slanted his lips over hers. She moaned as she was sandwiched tighter between the two men.

Hands on her hips held her in place as she closed her eyes and ran her hands up Johnny's chest. She wrapped her hands around his neck and pulled him tighter against her. Kevin's mouth latched onto the side of her neck and began sucking.

She moaned softly and opened her eyes. Derrick wasn't touching her. Why wasn't Derrick touching her? She looked around the kitchen for him. He stood a few feet away, leaning against the counter and watching the three of them.

She reached out to him, but he smirked and shook his head. She pouted, her bottom lip out.

"Oh no, baby girl." Derrick gave her a devilish grin, and she immediately knew she was dealing with Devil and not Derrick. "It's been too long since we've *played*." He gave her a pointed look. "On your knees."

She immediately lowered her eyes and let go of Johnny. Kevin and Johnny stepped back, and she gracefully slid to her knees between them. Once she was on her knees, she placed her upturned palms on her lap and slid her shoulders back. She kept her eyes lowered as she waited for his command.

"Such a good girl," Devil crooned, stepping toward her. He wrapped his hand around her jaw and lifted her chin. She kept her eyes lowered even as he lifted her face to his. "You've been working too hard."

She swallowed but kept quiet.

"It's been awhile since we've used this sexy little body as the cum dumpster it is," Devil said.

Heat flared inside her as a blush bloomed across her face and chest. Her pussy clenched and her lips parted as a soft gasp left her.

"Oh, you like that idea, do you?" He squeezed her jaw a little harder. "Are you still our little cum slut?"

She blushed as she nodded her head as much as she could with his grip on her jaw. "Yes, sir."

He laughed darkly. "Such a dirty little slut. She went and got herself knocked up."

Kara gasped and her eyes flew to his.

"Eyes down, slut," he ground out and roughly let go of her face.

She lowered her eyes and head at the same time, submitting to him.

"What are your safe words, slut?" Devil asked roughly.

"Green for good, yellow to slow down, and red to stop," she answered immediately.

"And you are?" he prompted.

"Green, sir, so green," she answered.

"Go upstairs and strip. I want you on your knees, your face down on the bed, your ass in the air. You will take your punishment without complaint."

"Yes, sir." Kara nodded and slowly rose to her feet.

She left the kitchen and headed upstairs. She could feel her arousal dripping already; her panties were soaked. She loved when her guys took control; she loved it even more when they got to play.

She stripped out of her work clothes and tossed them on the chair in the corner—she'd sort out her dry-clean only stuff later. She got in position at the foot of the bed. Up on her knees, she went down into child's pose and let the tension release from her body.

Each vertebra in her back aligned as she arched, then relaxed. She let out a soft breath and melted into the mattress. She wasn't sure how long she waited; she let herself drift into a meditative state, but she was nice and relaxed by the time she heard a soft creaking as the door was pushed open.

Her heart skipped in her chest at the promise of what was to come, and she had to force herself to remain calm and not move before her guys told her she could.

"Look at that, boys," Derrick crooned. "Such a wanton slut; that cunt is just dripping for a cock."

She heard them shuffle into the room behind her. A hand slid across her back and down her ass before it pulled away. There was a loud clap before the sharp stinging radiated from the slap to her ass. She breathed through her nose, proud of herself for not flinching.

"Too bad she only listens when she's about to get her cunt used," Kevin chided.

Butterflies fluttered in Kara's belly as she listened to the warning in Kevin's tone: they were about to play rough, and she was in for a long night.

"Time we remind her of her place, boys," Johnny said, his voice a deep rumble that sent shivers down her spine.

Just keep breathing. Kara forced herself to remain unflinching. With her forehead pressed against the mattress, she couldn't see anything. She could only guess as to what her boys were doing behind her.

She heard drawers slide; someone was digging through the nightstand next to the bed; her third guy was in the walk-in closet pulling out a tote. Shivers raced down her spine again—she knew what they kept in each of those places.

The bed dipped as someone knelt next to her. Fingers laced through her hair, fisted around her curly locks, and forcefully pulled her head up. She got a glimpse of Kevin before a soft blindfold was pulled over her eyes. Once it was settled in place, he let go of her hair roughly, and she fell back down onto the mattress. She caught herself with her hands and made the move more graceful as she slid back down into child's pose.

Someone gathered her thick curls—pulling them from around her face and over the strap of the blindfold—wrapping a hair tie around the mass of hair and tying it up in a ponytail.

A hand slid across her ass again, and she braced herself for another spank. When it didn't come, she couldn't relax. She knew they were up to something—this would be punishment, she knew. They didn't like her working so late anymore, not since she got pregnant.

"Up," Johnny ordered, his hand fisting into her ponytail to haul her upright on her knees. He stood behind her as she knelt at the edge of the bed. He roughly let go of her hair, and she swayed, trying to stay upright.

"Arms straight out in front of you," Derrick commanded from behind her.

Kara held her arms straight out from her body, moving her wrists together without needing to be told.

Derrick chuckled darkly. "You think if you're extra obedient right now we'll go easy on your punishment?"

Kara's spine stiffened as she froze in place. "No, I—" The spank to her ass effectively cut her off.

"You don't speak, slut," Derrick growled in her ear, his beard brushing over her smooth skin. *Devil*. She was no longer dealing with Derrick; Devil had taken the reins.

A shiver ran down her spine, but she didn't respond.

A moment later she felt the smooth texture of the silk Shibari rope slide over her biceps before a length of it was looped around her wrists. She held perfectly still while Derrick expertly wove the rope around her wrists and wrapped it up her forearms until he was pulling her arms up, above her head.

She let out a soft gasp as he pulled the rope taut and attached it to something on the ceiling. Did he have anchor hooks there? She hadn't noticed any before, but she couldn't remember the last time she paid any attention to the ceiling.

He pulled the rope so that she was forced to stay up on her knees, her back straight, while she tried not to put too much pressure on her shoulders. She shifted on her knees at the end of the bed, wondering just how in the hell she was going survive this one.

Something cold and wet touched her nipple, yanking her from her thoughts. She cried out and tried to jerk away, but whoever it was held the ice cube against her pebbled bud as another one was pressed to her other nipple.

She panted as she threw her head backward only for it to make contact with a rock-hard body. "Don't move," Kevin muttered in her ear. Where had Derrick gone?

Hands grabbed her hips and lifted her up while someone slid under her. She was lowered back down, now straddling thick thighs. Derrick's bushy beard brushed her nipple before he sucked it into his hot mouth. His hands slid from her hips up her back, sending shivers down her spine as the callouses skimmed over her soft skin. She moaned as Derrick pulled her body against his, and she shifted on the bed, making the rope around her wrists and arms pull tighter.

Derrick bit down on her sensitive nipple, and she gasped and tried to jerk away from him. He held her tighter as he lapped away the pain with his tongue.

Behind her, Kevin grabbed ahold of her ass cheeks and pulled them apart. She heard rustling in the corner of the room and the jingle of a chain, but the hands and mouth on her body took most of her focus.

Kevin leaned into her, pushing her further against Derrick, and sucked a bruising kiss into the side of her neck—that sweet spot they always homed in on.

She whimpered as softly as she could as the sensations drove her closer toward orgasm.

Kevin's fingers massaged her ass cheeks, pulling and kneading them like dough as he continued to suck a hickey into her neck.

She heard the jangle of a chain again—closer this time. She tensed as a calloused hand—Johnny's—wrapped around her ankle before she felt the cool metal of a bar being rested across the backs of both calves. Kevin's hands left her ass as he stepped back to allow Johnny room to fasten her ankles to the spreader bar.

Derrick moved to her other nipple, and Kara couldn't help but let out a low groan. The spreader bar held her knees far enough apart that she was forced by the rope to put more of her weight on her shoulders; she was mostly dangling from the rope now.

The bar was lifted, making her bend her knees until her ankles were touching the outsides of her thighs. Derrick pulled off her nipple with an audible pop before she felt another length of silk rope. Ever the rope master, Derrick wound a length around her thigh and calf, tying them together so she couldn't straighten her leg at all, before moving to her other leg. When he was finished, she was completely spread open and at the mercy of their advances.

The metal spreader bar hit the tops of her thighs below the curve of her ass, the cool metal quickly warming against her skin. Her nerves spiked, and she tilted her head back as if she'd be able to see the ceiling through the damn blindfold. They'd spoken about suspension play before...late at night, after they'd fucked, they had gone over things they'd be open to trying. Kara just never imagined it would be anything like this.

Someone grabbed the bar, pulling her away from Derrick so he could stand up. He brushed against her as he walked by, tweaking a nipple between his fingers as he passed. When they let go of the bar, she swung forward like a trapeze artist in a circus. Her weight was fully hanging from the ceiling, her knees barely brushing the mattress and slowing her swing just a little.

"Breathe." Kevin stepped in behind her, his breath hot on her ear as he wrapped his arms around her waist and held her against him. He took the weight off her shoulders just enough so she could relax in his arms. "You're doing amazing." He pressed a kiss to her shoulder and then gently let her go.

She took a calming breath and forced herself to relax. *You can do this.*

Kara didn't have to wait long before her guys were touching her again. She almost yelped at the cool, wet sensation of another ice cube—on her clit this time. She bit her lip to stifle her cry of surprise.

"Good girl," Derrick murmured from her left.

Heat rose and a blush spread on her chest and cheeks as his praise hit her harder than usual.

Derrick chuckled darkly. "Still our little praise skank."

"Goddamn, little slut." Johnny groaned. "You look fucking amazing."

She heard the click of a camera shutter and smiled. This may be her punishment, but she knew she looked damn good.

"I can't wait until this belly starts to grow," Kevin murmured as he rubbed his hands across her belly.

Derrick was still holding the ice cube to her clit, and she had to bite her lip again as he started circling the swollen nub, rubbing it gently until the ice melted completely.

"What do you say boys? Should we edge her tonight? Make her beg to come until she doesn't know her name anymore?" Kevin's hands slid up her belly and cupped her tender breasts harshly.

Kara whimpered quietly—remembering her order to stay quiet—as dark chuckles filled the room.

Kevin squeezed and kneaded her breasts, massaging them roughly. He pinched her nipples every so often, making her gasp.

"She's going to regret not listening to us about working so hard." Johnny laughed from her right before Kevin released her breasts and stepped away.

Someone's hand grabbed her thigh and roughly spun her in a circle. She cried out at the sudden movement, and a hand landed hot on her ass. "Quiet," Derrick growled.

She spun slowly back the other way as the rope unwound. There was a swooping sensation in her belly that had her heart racing as if she were on a roller coaster. Her pussy clenched down on nothing as her core throbbed. She was so fucking horny.

"Look at that drippy little cunt. She's absolutely weeping for a cock," Kevin crooned.

Kara forced herself not to whimper or beg. She heard the buzzing of a vibrator before she felt the strong vibrations of her magic wand against her clit. She tried to jerk away, but she had zero control over her body as it swung from the ceiling. No one touched her, only the magic wand buzzing against her clit.

She panted and gasped; she was already so fucking close.

"Do not come," Derrick ordered, his voice a sharp bark in her left ear.

She threw her head back and ground her teeth together, trying desperately to follow his order. But she was so damn close.

He pressed the wand harder against her clit, and her mouth dropped open in a silent cry. Tears welled in her eyes as she fought her body's response—fought the urge to come. Then the wand was pulled away and she gasped for breath, grateful for a reprieve.

Fingers immediately spread her ass cheeks apart, and lube was poured down her crack and over her puckered hole. "I'm going to fuck you until you're screaming, Princess," Johnny's low voice whispered in her ear as he stepped up against her backside.

His naked skin slid against hers, making her shiver. His thumbs pried open her cheeks as his large hands palmed her ass. He pulled her backward against him and nestled the head of his cock between her cheeks.

Someone slid against her front, and she heard the bed creak as they sat down on the edge. Johnny pressed into her ass, a slow thrust as he walked a step toward the bed, pushing her body forward so she was above the man sitting there.

Derrick's beard brushed her breast before he sucked her nipple into his mouth.

She was floating in her skin as if she were on ecstasy, every damn sensation only adding to her pleasure as sounds were muffled around her. Subspace was tugging her down, and she fell into it willingly, losing herself to the pleasure that rolled over her.

She felt herself being lowered as hands gripped her hips and guided her down onto Derrick's hard cock. "That's it, little slut." Derrick grunted as she was impaled on his dick.

Johnny pulled out of her before the spreader bar was uncuffed and removed, though her thighs and calves were still tied together. The rope holding her arms suspended was loosened and removed, though her wrists were still tied together. Johnny's hands slid up her sides to her arms, which he lowered and draped over Derrick's shoulders.

Johnny pushed her into Derrick, his large hand pressing between her shoulder blades until she was leaning against Derrick's front with Johnny glued to her back—sandwiching her between their two rock-hard bodies.

She let out a shuddering breath as her shoulders were allowed to relax.

Johnny massaged them as he thrust into her roughly. It was an odd sensation of pleasure and pain that overloaded her already disassociating brain. Shivers ran down her spine as she gasped quietly into the crook of Derrick's neck.

The bed dipped to her right before someone's hand fisted into her ponytail, turning her head roughly. "Suck it, slut," Kevin growled, pressing his cock against her lips.

She opened her mouth, unable to do more than run her tongue over his cock before he thrust deep into her mouth. Her body shuddered as an orgasm built again. She lay limply against Derrick with Kevin kneeling to her right, fucking her face as Derrick and Johnny fucked the rest of her holes.

"Fuck." Johnny groaned behind her.

"Yeah." Derrick grunted. He shifted beneath her, and she felt him wiggle his hand between their pressed bodies, sliding another ice cube between them and down to her clit. "Come for us, dirty slut."

Kara's loud cry was muffled around Kevin's cock as the ice cube pressed against her swollen clit. "Shit," Kevin muttered before spilling his cum down her throat.

Her body shuddered and tears leaked down her face as her orgasm crashed over her body, making her clamp down hard on Derrick's and Johnny's cocks. Kevin pulled out of her mouth, and she whimpered as her head fell down limply onto Derrick's shoulder.

Derrick and Johnny groaned as they followed her over the edge and came deep within her. Kara's entire body tingled and shook from the aftershocks of her orgasm as Johnny pulled out of her ass.

She must have dozed off, because when she came to a while later, she was no longer tied up and hands were massaging her everywhere, rubbing her arms and wrists, thighs and calves. She was lying face down in the middle of the bed, and they were using massage oil as they rubbed her gently.

She moaned faintly and opened her eyes. The room was dimly lit, but she could make out each of her guys easily. "Hi beautiful."

Kevin smiled widely before he leaned down and pressed a gentle kiss to her lips.

She grinned and yawned deeply, letting out another moan.

"How you doing, baby girl?" Derrick asked from behind her.

"So fucking good," she mumbled, closing her eyes again.

"You need to drink some water before you go back to sleep, Princess," Johnny murmured before he pressed a kiss between her shoulder blades. He nudged her side before he gently rolled her over.

She blinked up at him. He was straddling her waist, a pair of boxer briefs covering his body. Her arm was uncoordinated as she tried to reach out for him, her weak muscles making her fall short.

He took pity on her and leaned down over her.

"Mmm," she murmured, smiling as she managed to slide her hand around the back of his neck and pull him into a sloppy kiss.

He chuckled as he lowered himself down against her body, resting his weight on his elbows on either side of her head so as not to crush her completely.

They made out lazily while she slowly regained control of her body and came back into herself. Her heart was light—she'd never been so happy in all her life.

"Fucking hell, baby girl." Derrick groaned.

She smiled into the kiss with Johnny before he chuckled and pulled away, climbing off her completely. "Time for bed, Princess."

She hummed, smiling, and turned to Kevin. She crooked her finger at him in a come-hither motion.

He laughed but crawled up the bed until he was lying on his side, head propped up on his elbow. "Hi, love."

She hummed again and reached out for him. He cupped her jaw in his large hand as he guided her mouth to his. They kissed sensually for several moments before he pulled away from her. "I love you."

"Mmm, love you too." She moaned as he rolled away from her. She turned, looking for Derrick, and grinned when she found him already crawling toward her.

His long brown hair was tied back in a low ponytail, and his green eyes sparkled with mischief as he lowered himself over her naked body. "Hi, baby girl."

"Hi, lover boy." She threaded her fingers through his hair and pulled him down to kiss her. He lowered his body onto hers, resting his full weight against hers. She sighed happily into the kiss and wrapped her other arm around his back.

"So good for us," he murmured as he pulled back.

She smiled as he pressed a kiss to her forehead before he climbed off her. Johnny returned and gently slid a warm washcloth through her folds, cleaning her. "Do you want to shower before bed?"

She shook her head as her eyelids fluttered shut.

"Not yet, babe," Kevin murmured and patted her shoulder. "Up here."

She opened her eyes and turned to see what he meant; she was lying in the middle of their extra-large bed, and Kevin was pointing toward the headboard and pillows. She sighed and rolled onto her side. She slowly crawled up the mattress to where Kevin had already turned down the sheets and blankets.

"Water," Derrick said, holding her stainless steel cup toward her, straw poised at her lips. She sighed as she sipped the cool water, eyes fluttering.

"Thanks," she murmured when she was done. She slipped under the cool sheets, naked, and let out a content sigh as her head hit the pillow. "Love you," she muttered to her guys before she closed her eyes and drifted off to sleep.

# Chapter Fifteen

I T WAS LATE WHEN the phone rang. Johnny rolled over and glanced at the clock as he reached for his cell: one thirty a.m. It was never good news when the phone rang in the middle the night. He grabbed his phone and quickly sat up when he saw the name on the screen.

"Marcos," Johnny greeted with a growl.

"Hey man, sorry to wake you. We've got Buckley tied up in the basement," Marcos explained immediately. "My club voted. He's yours if you want him."

That was *not* what Johnny expected to come out of Marcos's mouth. "What happened?" Johnny asked, rubbing a hand over his buzzed hair.

"He killed a brother tonight. Was too drugged out to realize and shot him in the middle of the clubhouse during a party." Marcos sighed.

Johnny paused, still half asleep and wondering if he'd heard him correctly. "I'll talk to my club in the morning. Give you a call when I know what's going on," Johnny said, unable to make a club decision unilaterally.

"Roger that," Marcos said before he hung up.

Johnny sighed and put his phone back on the nightstand. He glanced over his shoulder at the extra-large bed, at the three sleeping bodies that lay there, but a set of bright blue eyes awake and shining in the light of the bathroom nightlight.

Johnny laid back down and rolled toward Kara. He slid an arm under her head and the other between her legs, grabbing ahold of her ass and pulling her against his body. Once she was wrapped around him, and he around her, he took a deep breath and snuggled into her neck. "Your brother called. He wants to set up a truce between the clubs."

Kara breathed a sigh of relief and melted into his body. "Will the Knights go for that?" she asked softly, knowing it wasn't just up to him.

"I think so. We've already laid it all on the table for them; they just need to vote on it," Johnny explained. "Marcos wants the clubs to meet."

Kara nodded against his chest. "Where?"

"I don't know. I need to find somewhere neutral."

"Slade's?" Kara suggested.

Johnny shook his head. "She won't allow the Psychos there after Rachet...and it's not big enough."

Kara sighed and rubbed a hand down Johnny's back. Her nails lightly grazed his skin and a slight shiver went down his spine. He fucking loved how her touch could drive him up the wall. "You'll figure it out, baby," she murmured, her voice soft, half asleep.

He pressed a kiss to her forehead and ran his own hand down her bare back. He couldn't remember the last time she had worn clothing to bed. If she did, it was quickly discarded by one of them.

Since the new bed had been delivered, Kevin and Derrick hadn't slept in their own rooms. That was fine with Johnny. He didn't mind sharing with them—his brothers—they had shared everything for decades now. It was a comfort to roll over and know his brother was there and had his back.

Johnny drifted off to sleep with his girl in his arms and his brothers on his mind.

In the end, Johnny decided to host the Devil's Psychos at his home. He needed someplace neutral and large enough to hold everyone.

It might not have been completely neutral ground, but it wasn't like he hosted his own club at his house often either.

"Thanks, man," Marcos greeted when he rolled up with half his club.

His two best friends Stone and Dagger were by his side along with two old-timers that Johnny only knew by face, not by name.

Johnny nodded as he shook Marcos's hand. "What better way to show trust than to invite you into my home?"

"This is your place?" Dagger asked, his eyes roaming over the large house.

Johnny nodded and crossed his arms, Derrick and Kevin at his back. "We built it together," he answered.

"Holy shit, man," Dagger huffed and moved down the driveway. "Can I check out the back?" he asked.

Johnny chuckled and shared a look with Marcos. "He's special," Marcos replied.

Stone laughed. "He's got a thing for architecture." He shrugged.

Soon enough, everyone from both clubs had rolled up, lining the driveway with dozens of bikes. Johnny had opened up the backyard bar shed that was just off the pool and had even brought over a couple bartenders from the clubhouse.

Music played through the backyard speakers, a fire roared in the firepit, and dozens of bikers shuffled around his backyard, talking in groups. The grill was cranking, and a chef from the clubhouse restaurant was there, utilizing Johnny's grill and kitchen to feed dinner to everyone.

Johnny hoped his wining and dining would pay off. He hoped that everything he had laid out to his own club would pay off. It already sounded like the Psychos were on board, but he could tell some were still leery of an outright truce, and Johnny knew damn well that the Ravager Knights did NOT trust the Devil's Psychos. At least most of them. Even with all the drinks poured throughout the evening, he could still see tensions were high, but there were small pockets where the two clubs interacted.

It all changed when Kara came home as dinner was being served. The men were just sitting down at the tables scattered around the backyard when Kara walked out back. She was still dressed in her work clothes—a formfitting dress in a deep green color—having come from a weekend meeting with Winters.

She smiled as she looked around the yard. When her eyes met his, her smile grew brighter, if possible, and she headed toward him at the head of one of the tables. Rockstar and Devil sat on his right side, Marcos on his left. Stone and Dagger sat next to Marcos in a showing of trust and strength.

"Hey, Princess," Johnny greeted as she rounded the table. She greeted Derrick with a quick peck to the lips, then Kevin, who held her against him longer before she slid onto Johnny's lap with a smile. He gave her a lingering kiss that had Marcos clearing his throat.

"Hey, brother," Kara murmured and kissed Johnny again. She held out her hand to Marcos, and they did a complicated handshake consisting of lots of slapping and sliding of palms, all while Kara was engrossed in kissing Johnny.

"Really?" Marcos asked, sounding incredulous.

There was a smattering of laughter around the yard.

Kara pulled away, breathless, and turned to her brother with a flushed face and a smile. "Hi, big brother," she greeted him properly.

He rolled his eyes. "Hi, little sister."

Stone and Dagger chuckled next to him.

Kara turned to them and smiled widely. "Hi Jason, Nico." She slid off Johnny's lap and rounded the table behind Marcos and greeted his friends. Stone and Dagger both stood up and gave her hugs.

"What the shit?" Marcos grumbled. "They get hugs, but I get some half-assed handshake while you sucked his face?"

Kara laughed heartily. "Yeah, brother. I'm still annoyed with you."

Marcos rolled his eyes but stood up and turned to Kara as she let go of Stone. She smiled as she leaned in and hugged him tightly. "Hi, Marquitos." She sighed.

"Hola, lil *Manita*," Marcos murmured before he leaned back and pressed a kiss to the top of her head.

Johnny watched while also taking in the men surrounding them. The members of the two clubs were also taking in the scene between the VP and his sister, a tender moment between family that Marcos wasn't afraid to be part of in front of everyone.

Johnny's respect for Marcos only grew as he gave his sister a soft smile and as Kara slid back onto Johnny's knee.

"Let me get you a drink," Dagger said, moving to stand back up.

"No, I'm OK." Kara smiled as Kevin slid over an unopened bottle of water.

"Nah," Dagger said. "We're all drinking your Macallan. We should get you one."

Kara shook her head. "I can't." She shrugged.

Johnny smirked as he watched Stone freeze, his eyes flying to Kara's. Marcos smiled softly as he watched the two of them bicker.

Dagger was a little slower on the uptake. "Nonsense. You can have a drink with us before we get to business."

Kara smiled wider. "I can't drink, Nic," she said soundly.

More eyes turned their way, taking in the scene.

Dagger was half out of his chair when he finally turned back to Kara, as if finally registering what she was trying to tell him. "What do you mean, you *can't* drink?" he growled, staring at Kara.

Kara's smile grew brighter. "Like I said, Nico," she leaned back against Johnny's chest, and he wrapped his arms around her and rested one hand on her belly, "I can't drink alcohol anymore."

"Holy shit." Dagger gasped, falling back into his chair. "Are you pregnant?"

Kara giggled seeing the utter disbelief and amazement on her friend's face and nodded.

"Holy shit!" Dagger repeated, this time louder. He officially had gained the attention of every single person in the backyard. "I'm gonna be an uncle?" he asked, a shit-eating grin spread over his face.

"Yeah." Kara laughed.

"FUCK YEAH," he yelled and sprang to his feet. He pulled Kara off Johnny's lap and into his arms. He wrapped her in a hug and lifted her, spinning around, laughing, and shouting, "I'M GONNA BE AN UNCLE!"

Loud cheering and clapping started as congratulations were shouted all around.

"Dude, fuck off!" Marcos shouted at his buddy, a wide smile on his face. "I'm the uncle; you're just the monkey."

Dagger shot Marcos the bird behind Kara's back as he held her tightly. Clearly, he thought of Kara as a little sister as well.

Johnny had a broad grin on his face that he shared with Kevin and Derrick and nodded. Johnny felt a lot more confident in his personal decision to partner with Marcos and the Psychos. His club still had to vote on it, but if there was one thing he knew about his club, it was that they put family first. They would embrace Kara's pregnancy and vote for the alliance because Johnny's kid would bind the clubs together.

When Dagger finally put Kara back on her feet, there were tears in both their eyes. Dagger quickly blinked his away, but Kara let a couple fall and made a show of wiping them away.

"Congratulations again, sister," Marcos said softly. He stood up and pulled her into a tight hug.

"Thanks, brother." She nodded, a watery smile in place.

"Let's celebrate! Shots!" Dagger shouted with a smile.

Kara laughed and turned back to Johnny. She pressed a kiss to his lips. "I'm gonna head in," she murmured against his lips.

"Alright, Princess," he murmured, pulling her tight against him. "Don't wait up for us," he said gruffly.

She nodded and pressed another kiss to his lips. "I love you."

"Love you too, Princess."

Johnny pulled away from Kara so she could kiss Kevin and Derrick. Johnny made sure she was inside the house before he turned back to the party around him. With Kara safely in the house, his brothers and the Devil's Psychos moved in and patted him on the back, offering him congratulations.

As the night progressed, the fire in the pit grew to the size of a raging bonfire. Old pallets were thrown on top along with other shit brought home from jobsites.

"Alright, alright!" Johnny shouted over the boisterous crowd sometime later.

He'd already spoken to most of the members of his club privately after dinner, so he was confident that when he called to attention the group of men before him, there wouldn't be any surprise votes.

"I wanna thank all you assholes for coming out tonight." Johnny started his speech once he had everyone's attention. He smirked as middle fingers were raised and boos were shouted from both clubs. "On a serious note, though," Johnny slowed his speech and paused slightly, gearing up for the more serious talk he needed to give, "we've gone through some shit the last several weeks. Tensions have been high, and a war was started." He paused again to take in the men around him. He appraised the mood and assessed tempers as men shifted in their boots. "An unfounded war to line the pockets of the already filthy rich. Vince Carmichael used the Devil's Psychos as he used King Taylor, as just another pawn in a rich man's game." Again, Johnny paused. He looked around the group of men before him and felt it in his soul: this was his family, all of them. "While Larry Buckley and Vince Carmichael might have started this war, blood was still spilled, and Ravager Knights were killed." Johnny took in the eyes on him. Men stood still as they gave him their undivided attention. "For there to be peace, there needs to be retribution."

Murmurs rippled around the bonfire, and men grumbled their agreement. An edge of violence crept into the crowd.

Marcos stepped forward and looked around at the men gathered there. He made eye contact with his brothers before he finally turned to Johnny. "I wanna thank you," he started, speaking clearly and slowly for all those watching, "for inviting the Devil's Psychos into your home. You showed great trust when you invited us here, and I appreciate that. My brothers appreciate that." Marcos paused and scratched his eyebrow with a middle finger. "Most people don't know this," he chuckled faintly, "but my sister Kara called me several months ago. She wanted to tell me about the new relationship she was in and the guys she had met." Marcos laughed again. "You can imagine my surprise when she told me there were three of them."

The group of men laughed, well acquainted with Kara's relationship with Johnny, Kevin, and Derrick.

"After I got over my initial shock," Marcos smiled, "she told me about how her own father, a man who's been a thorn in my side for the last nine years, was framing King Taylor for a laundry list of shit he didn't do. Then she told me she was going to help represent King Taylor in court against her own father because King was innocent."

Mutters rang out around the fire; men grumbled and shifted. "We all know Vince Carmichael was using the Devil's Psychos to start a war to kill Mac Taylor," Marcos continued. "Buckley was not only working with Vince Carmichael behind the backs of the

Devil's Psychos, he was working with Las Serpientes as well. Our own sworn enemy."

Growls and grumbles were spat around the fire from both clubs.

"As vice president of the Devil's Psychos and acting president until further notice, I offer the Ravager Knights our president, Larry 'The Butcher' Buckley, as payment and retribution for the war that was wrongfully fired up between our clubs. I offer him up as a first step of alliance between our clubs." Marcos finished and turned to look at Johnny with a nod, stretching his hand out to the Ravager Knights president and waiting.

Johnny nodded slowly and turned to his own club. "I ask you, my brothers," making eye contact with each one of them, "to vote for a truce, vote now for peace and to end this war, vote for a united front against the fucking serpents and their dirty deals. Vote so our families can thrive together. What do you say?"

He'd barely finished speaking before the *ayes* rang out loud and clear. Mammoth and Vagabond, Hotrod and Welder, Lemmy, Darrel, and Bandit. They all voted yes.

A vengeful grin pulled at Johnny's lips as he turned to Marcos and his still-outstretched hand. "You hand over Buckley, and you have yourself an alliance and a truce," Johnny said.

"You have my word." Marcos nodded once.

Johnny slapped his hand into Marcos's and shook it tightly. "It's a deal."

Cheers went up around the fire, and Marcos stepped in, slipping their hands from a formal shake to a brotherly half hug. He slapped Johnny on the back and muttered so only he could hear. "I want Carmichael though," Marcos declared, his eyes fierce in the firelight.

Johnny ground his teeth and nodded once.

At the end of the day, he didn't care who took out Vince Carmichael as long as he went down the same way his father had: murdered in cold blood.

K ARA WAS WOKEN IN the early morning to loud cheering and yelling from the backyard through an open window in the master bedroom. She knew what that cheer meant: the alliance between the clubs had been formed.

A sense of calm washed over her knowing her brother and boyfriends would be safe and no longer in danger of killing one another. It was a weight lifted off her shoulders.

Kara drifted off to sleep for another hour before she heard the rumbles of bikes starting up. A lot of bikes, all of the bikes.

She groaned and rolled over. She rubbed a hand over her face, knowing what piece of retribution had been on the table for this truce and alliance to go through.

Larry Buckley's head on a spike.

Maybe not so literally, but he would be dead. And by the sounds of the bikes revving up outside, he would be dead soon.

Kara rolled out of bed, stood up, pulled a random T-shirt over her head, and headed for the bedroom window that overlooked the driveway and garage. The spotlights and coach lights on the garage lit up the group of bikers who were gearing up and getting ready to depart. She found her three men, four if she included her brother, standing in the well-lit garage.

As if sensing her at the window, all four of them looked up at her.

She pressed two fingers to her lips, kissed them, then slowly pulled them away, less like she was blowing a kiss and more like a salute. "*Abrazos de la Muerte*," she muttered, almost as a prayer.

Death's embrace.

It was something Marcos and Kara had learned growing up in Creekton, a saying they had heard in passing and made their own. Death came for all, and it was only a matter of time before he came for you too.

Kara watched Marcos lift two fingers and press them to his lips. He saluted her back, and she watched his lips form the words. "*Abrazos de la Muerte.*"

After a quick discussion, her three large and deadly men—her boys—each met her gaze and lifted their fingers to their lips. As one they kissed their fingers and saluted her before each one of them repeated the phrase.

It was a promise. An acknowledgment to be careful. A show of love.

She nodded to them, then turned away from the window and climbed back into bed, shrugging off the T-shirt and tossing it to the floor.

The ride to the Devil's Psychos clubhouse wasn't long. The night air whipped around Johnny as the roar of the pack of motorcycles screamed down the highway.

Marcos rode at his side, Rockstar and Stone behind them.

This was one of the pivotal moments in life, one when you knew life would be forever changed afterward. The path he was heading on was a dark one, but there was a light at the end of the tunnel that would hopefully lead to a peaceful union.

They headed south on Route 45 for another ten minutes before they passed the Seratelli casino: Stella's. It was on the left side of the road, on the border between Creekton and Mourningside. A riverboat casino right on the Evermore River, it was lit up as bright as the sun in the twilight. Across the street from it was a large ongoing high-rise project—the Seratellis' new hotel—and around it, a bustling lineup of businesses, all owned by the Seratellis, had cropped up on an otherwise vacant road.

A moment later, they passed the sign welcoming visitors to Creekton. The main street heading into the city was hopping—even in the early hours of the morning—with the patrons of gentleman's clubs and bars, all in line with what the Seratellis were building just outside the city limits.

They turned off the main drag a moment later and followed a winding road along the river. They eventually turned back toward Main Street, and Johnny could see the club's old motel and restaurant, set a couple buildings in from the main drag, on Drauden. It was set far enough away from the central road that its location was probably what killed it back in its heyday. Now it was the perfect place for an outlaw gang of bikers to hide in plain sight.

Johnny followed Marcos into the parking lot, and they quickly lined up the bikes. He didn't plan on staying long; he really didn't see the point. He was here for retribution: kill Buckley and end the war. Besides, he had a sexy blond at home in his bed.

Marcos didn't waste any time. He gave Johnny a nod and headed for the clubhouse doors. Johnny followed, with Rockstar and Stone behind him. They would keep formation until they reached their destination.

Marcos headed straight through the clubhouse, ignoring everyone. There was a small gathering of people hanging around. "Out," Marcos ordered and headed for a door in the back.

Johnny glanced back over his shoulder to see his own club filing inside the clubhouse with the rest of the Psychos. The group of people hanging around quickly trooped out the door, past the club members.

Once everything was locked down and closed up, Marcos opened a steel door and headed down a set of stairs behind it. Johnny followed him into the basement. The smell of damp earth rose up to greet them. Damp earth and piss.

The basement was dimly lit. A single bulb hung from the center of the room. Several small jail cells were built against one cinder-block wall.

A lump of a man lay propped against the cinder blocks. His long white hair was stringy about his face; his white shirt was sweat stained. His beer gut rose and fell with the effort it took to bring air into his lungs as he panted shallowly.

Johnny thought he'd heard a rumor about Buckley's needing oxygen.

In short, President Larry "The Butcher" Buckley, of the Devil's Psychos Motorcycle Club, looked like utter shit.

A cruel smirk twisted at Johnny's lips as he took in the utter disgrace of the man sprawled out before him.

Buckley laughed low as both clubs formed a semicircle around the cell. "Well, well, well," Buckley wheezed. "If it ain't the band of pussies and their fearless leader, Mayhem," Buckley taunted.

Johnny growled low in his throat. "The fuck you say to me?"

Buckley laughed softly again, but it turned into a wheezing cough as he struggled to catch his breath.

Johnny sneered at the man. "Looks like you could use your oxygen, old man," Johnny taunted.

When Buckley could only cough, Johnny motioned at him. "I need him to answer a couple questions first."

Marcos signaled to the patched brother that had been guarding Buckley when they walked in. The man looked vaguely familiar. Johnny watched him move a large oxygen tank on wheels over to the jail cell and unravel the clear tubing.

Buckley made a desperate lunge toward the cell bars and pulled the clear tube and mask up to his face. He took deep, gasping breaths as he gulped down air.

It was pathetic to see such a piece of shit already on death's door. Johnny had half a mind to let the man live out his miserable existence in the basement, slowly suffocating.

"Why were you working with Vince Carmichael?" Johnny asked, his voice hard as steel.

Buckley laughed. "'Cause he was a snake and wanted the same shit I did: Mac Taylor dead."

"Why?" Johnny demanded.

"Why not? Fucking Taylor rode around here making deals with the Tarazovs and stirring shit up with the Seratellis, acting like he owned fucking Creekton and Mourningside too. I was fucking sick of it." Buckley spat.

Johnny's eyebrows furrowed together. He glanced at Nico. Nic shook his head slightly; he had no idea. "What kind of deals with the Seratellis?" Johnny asked.

"The kind that blow up the fucking coke trade from Chicago to Birmingham," Buckley growled.

It fucking dawned on Johnny right then: the Devil's Psychos had attacked them in Alabama, along the trade routes. They'd killed Rachet because Mac was making deals with the Mafia to move coke.

Rage boiled in his chest.

"Where is Vince Carmichael?" Johnny growled.

Buckley laughed deeply. "Fuck if I know. Asshole only came round to throw money around. He was paying me to start a war with the Knights; he rarely told me shit."

Hisses of rage zipped around the semicircle.

Johnny locked his jaw, grinding his molars as he glared down at the piece of shit in front of him. He believed him. Looking at Buckley now, the man had no plays up his sleeve; he had no more information Johnny needed.

Any questions he had could only be answered by his father, and that wasn't possible.

Johnny motioned toward the cell door.

Marcos walked over and unlocked it.

Johnny pulled a nine-millimeter Beretta from its holster under his arm, concealed by his cut. He stepped into the cell, gun aimed at his target, and Buckley laughed again. "I should have fucked your little whore—"

Johnny pulled the trigger.

Blood and brain matter splattered on the cinder-block wall behind Buckley. A single bullet hole, between Buckley's unseeing eyes, was all it took to end the life of the man who had been a thorn in his side for years.

"*Abrazos de la Muerte*," Johnny muttered. He thought when Buckley died that he would feel relieved, thought he would feel a sense of peace wash over him.

Instead, he felt nothing, not even numb.

He nodded once at Marcos, then turned and walked out of the cell. He walked up the basement stairs and out of the clubhouse without a backward glance.

He had done what he'd come to do. The war was over. Peace could reign. And Johnny had the love of his life waiting for him in his bed.

Chapter Seventeen

K ARA WOKE TO THE mattress dipping on either side of her. Three sets of hands found her body in the dark and slid rough calloused hands over her warm, smooth, naked skin. She woke slowly as mouths soon joined the hands on her body.

She'd gone back to bed naked, knowing her men would slide in when they came home.

The sheet was pulled slowly from her body, exposing her supple flesh to the cool air. Warm hands and mouths quickly heated her with sensual touches. She moaned as a mouth closed around her nipple, sucking and nibbling. Hands slid down her sides, grabbing and massaging her ass cheeks, parting the thick globes. She moaned, and lips found hers in the darkness and sucked down her moans in a sloppy kiss. *Derrick*.

Fingers parted her folds and slid into her.

She opened her eyes, but darkness had engulfed the room; the blackout curtains were pulled tight, belying the fact it was early morning and starting to lighten outside. She let her eyes fall closed again as Derrick's kiss grew filthier, his beard tickling her skin as his tongue fucked into her mouth at a slow and leisurely pace.

The hands spreading her ass cheeks yanked her down the bed and ripped her away from Derrick's kiss. A cock speared into her in one hard thrust that left her breathless. Another mouth claimed hers as its owner leaned over and covered her body with his. *Johnny*. His beard was shorter and softer. She felt his elbows brace on the mattress on either side of her head.

He fucked her slowly. Kissed her sensually.

Derrick and Kevin backed off, and only Johnny touched her. He rocked into her. His kiss dominated her.

She clung to his back as he chipped away at her heart and soul. No words were needed as he poured his love for her into his lovemaking.

It wasn't long before she was arching against him, her cries of passion being drowned in his kiss. He didn't stop, didn't slow. He rode her slowly through her orgasm until she was a gasping, writhing mess beneath him.

Johnny's hand fisted in her hair as he kissed her roughly, sucking the breath from her and leaving her panting. When he finally broke it off to let her breathe, he kissed down her jawline and into the crook of her neck.

She arched for him and gave him more access.

He snapped his hips faster and picked up his pace. He reached between them and circled her clit with his fingers. "Come for me, Princess," he ordered into her ear.

It sent chills racing down her spine. She spread her legs wider and shifted her hips so his pubic bone was rubbing over her clit as the same time his fingers were toying with her. She arched her back and groaned deeply as another orgasm ripped out of her.

She clamped down on his cock, and he groaned. She held onto him tightly as he picked up the pace and followed her over the edge.

They lay there panting softly for a moment before Johnny lifted up onto his elbows. He placed a sensual kiss to her lips before he slid out.

Kevin took his place, sliding inside her without warning. She was already so soaked with her own fluids and Johnny's cum that Kevin slid in easily. She moaned and wrapped her arms around him, pulling him in tight. "So perfect, baby," he muttered against her lips.

She smiled lazily and let him lead.

He made love to her slowly and sensually. Tears cascaded down her face as he poured his soul into making love to her. "So damn beautiful." He smiled and kissed her.

She moaned into the kiss and held on tight as he snapped his hips more sharply and hit her clit just right. The orgasm rolled over her in slow and sensual waves. Her walls clamped down on him as she arched against him.

He groaned and picked up his pace. Breaking the kiss, he dropped his head into the crook of her neck. "Fuck." He moaned as he came.

Kara was so relaxed, so exhausted she barely registered when Kevin rolled off her and slid over on the mattress so Derrick could take his place.

"Hey, baby girl," Derrick murmured against her lips before he claimed them with his own. He slid into her and got right to moving. She gasped and angled them so her clit hit his pubic bone with every thrust. She was so sensitive already, so relaxed, when the orgasm hit her, she shuddered and tried to push him away.

Derrick shook his head and laced their fingers together. He pulled her arms over her head and held them loosely. His hips twisted and pumped into her a couple times before he, too, was following her over the edge with a low groan.

All three of her guys were so intent on making love to her. They showered her with orgasms and showed their love through touch. She knew the night had been hard for them, chasing down

Buckley. But she was glad it was over, glad they could move on together.

She smiled lazily and drifted off to sleep before Derrick could even slide out of her. She'd never been so sated and relaxed in her life.

Despite the alliance between the Devil's Psychos and the Ravager Knights, Kara felt almost a sense of urgency settle on her shoulders in the weeks following Buckley's death. Things were calm between the clubs and life seemed almost normal, but she felt like the walls were closing in.

She needed to find her father. She needed an address for his place in the Caymans.

Short of going down there and looking through public records, she was at a loss for how to find him. So she started combing through files at the office again, looking for any scrap piece of paper that might have an address scribbled on it or, if she was lucky, the deed to the place.

With Vince officially on the run, Johnny had club members stationed outside her father's house, keeping a lookout.

Kara and her guys had already searched through her father's house on multiple occasions, looking for a lead. Or a safe. They found neither.

Kara was hitting wall after wall of dead ends, and it was grating on her nerves. When she wasn't in the office, she was seeing the physical therapist for her wrist and her knee. Though both were doing well, she still had a couple more weeks before the doctor would clear her officially. Even then, her knee might give her problems for the rest of her life if she didn't stay active.

All of it led back to her father's being a piece of shit.

Her phone rang, pulling her from her thoughts as she dug through dusty boxes in her office. A quick glance at the screen showed it was Derrick. "Hey," she greeted while sliding the phone between her ear and shoulder.

"Baby girl, what are you wearing?" Derrick's rough and tumble voice was low and playful.

She smiled easily and glanced down. "Khakis," she deadpanned.

He laughed deeply. "Johnny's sending me down to the county clerk's office to pick up a couple building plans for some projects coming up. You wanna go for a ride?"

"Fuck yes." She grinned, dropping the papers she was digging through. She stood up and glanced down at the skirt and blouse she had on.

"So what are you really wearing?" he asked, pressing the issue again, not just being sexy this time. Her boys were all about motorcycle safety when it came to her, and pantyhose, a skirt, and heels were not *smart* choices for riding bitch on a motorcycle. She had been OK with a similar outfit during Mac's funeral as they'd ridden slowly, but the pregnancy put everything under a microscope, and she found herself overanalyzing constantly.

"I have clothes with me," she told Derrick. "I'll change and be right down. Meet you in the lobby in ten?"

"Make it five, baby girl. I'm hungry." He growled before he disconnected.

She rolled her eyes and hung up, grabbing her bag of spare clothes from her work closet, then heading for her attached bathroom, a perk of being the managing partner.

She made quick work of slipping into a pair of ripped jeans. She left her pantyhose on underneath so the black hose showed through the holes in the denim. She exchanged the blouse for a plain black T-shirt and her black leather jacket. She'd taken to wearing it everywhere she could, only changing into suit coats when she got to the office.

She was in the process of tying up her black combat boots when her phone rang again. "I'm coming," she snipped at Derrick.

"Not yet you aren't, but you will be," he snapped back at her.

She grinned. "On my way." She ended the call and quickly finished her task.

By the time she was downstairs in the lobby, Derrick was out front on his motorcycle, parked by the front doors.

She shook her head at his impatience and waved to Trevor, the security guard. "Bye T. Have a good night."

"Alright Miss Carmichael. You take care of yourself now," the large Jamaican man said with a smile.

Kara pushed through the revolving door and headed out into the crisp late September afternoon. Fall was settling into Illinois, and winter would soon be right behind it. Kara didn't know how much longer she would be riding with her boys, but for the time being, while she could, she would enjoy every moment of it.

"You're late," Derrick greeted her, raising an eyebrow. He had his arms crossed over his chest as he leaned back against his motorcycle. His black Taylor Construction T-shirt was stretched tight across his muscular chest. His beard was about an inch long, recently trimmed so he looked less like a caveman and more like a lumberjack.

She smirked and slinked toward him. "You starving, baby?" she asked, lowering her voice and sashaying her hips as she approached him.

He grinned wickedly and grabbed her hips. She stepped between his spread legs and leaned into him. "You have no idea." His voice was a low rumble in his chest.

"I've got something you can eat," she teased, watching his green eyes darken with desire.

"I plan to," he shot back. "Keep it up, and I might just bend you over this bike and do it right where anyone can see."

She blushed and bit her lip.

"I see you like that idea." He grinned. His hands slid slowly from her hips, up her sides, over her belly, and up to her breasts, which he cupped gently. "And how are these feeling today?" he asked.

She groaned, arching her back. "They're sore," she admitted. At the three-month mark, things were starting to change a bit with her body. The nausea was mostly gone, thank God, but her breasts were starting to grow in size and sensitivity.

"We'll have to make sure to massage them extra good tonight," Derrick crooned and pressed a kiss to her lips.

She smiled and leaned into him. His hands slid down her sides and back to her hips again. He pulled her against him and kissed her soundly. When she broke away breathless a moment later, she rubbed a hand over his beard and jaw. "Why are we going to the county clerk's office?" she asked.

"'Cause we got a couple old house projects coming up. Johnny needs the blueprints," Derrick answered.

"And the county clerk has the blueprints?" she furrowed her eyebrows together, feeling slow on the uptake.

"Blueprints are public record. They have them for all buildings. You just have to ask for a copy," Derrick said.

Kara nodded slowly, understanding what he said while slowly realizing the piece she was missing. "That's it!" she exclaimed. "The blueprints! We need the blueprints for my father's house! Then we can see what we're missing!"

A shocked grin spread across Derrick's face. "Holy shit, baby girl! That's genius!" He wrapped his arms around her and lifted her up into a bone-crushing hug.

She held on tight, hugging him back just as fiercely. Excitement coursed through her, easing some of her anxiety over the case. "Come on, baby daddy. Let's get out of here."

He laughed and let out a whoop of delight. He spun her one more time before he set her back on her feet and climbed on the bike. He waited until she was seated safely behind him to start the engine.

The ride from the Carmichael building downtown to the county clerk's office took thirty minutes in the late-afternoon traffic. They made it to the courthouse with roughly an hour to spare.

Kara glanced down and cursed her choice of clothing. The county clerk's building was attached to Mourningside County Courthouse, which was always a bustling place, even at four on a Wednesday night.

"You look hot, baby girl. Don't worry." Derrick smiled. He flung an arm around her shoulders and tucked her into his side as they took the long sidewalk to the main entrance.

Kara sighed. She could only hope she didn't run into anyone she worked with regularly. If they were lucky, they would be in and out in under an hour.

They made it through security without a fuss. She didn't see any of the usual security guards she knew from the day shift. The building records were kept in the basement of the clerk's building, a place Kara had never been before.

Derrick seemed to know where he was going, though, so she followed his lead. He kept his fingers laced with hers as they walked.

"Carmichael?" a female voice asked just as they entered the records department.

Kara sighed, closing her eyes for a moment to steel herself before she opened them and turned. "Holy shit." She gasped, utterly shocked by who she saw. "Lizzie Braidwell. Holy fuck, girl, you look amazing." Kara released Derrick's hand to make a beeline for her old high school friend, greeting her with a broad smile and a huge hug.

"Damn girl." Lizzie laughed. "You look fucking hot."

Kara laughed and hugged her old friend tighter. "How the hell have you been?" Kara asked when she eventually pulled away. She looked over her friend, taking everything in.

Lizzie was slightly taller than Kara's five feet three, and she had hazel eyes that bordered on a sea green most of the time. Her light brown hair came down just below her shoulders and was high-lighted with bright blond streaks and curled into big voluminous waves. She had almost the same build as Kara and was confidently rocking an all-white business suit. She looked spectacular.

"I've been good," Lizzie answered with a smile. "You know how life gets so busy after high school and college."

"Oh my God, tell me about it." Kara laughed. "Most days I'm swamped and don't know which end is up anymore."

"I bet," Lizzie said, still smiling, though that faded with her next words. "I've been following the news about your dad."

"Yeah. It's been rough." Kara sighed and nodded. "It's part of why we're here. I was hoping to get blueprints of my father's house, and my boyfriend needs some blueprints for a couple projects he's going be starting soon." She motioned toward Derrick.

"I can totally help with that!" Lizzie grinned. "Hi, I'm Lizzie. I went to high school with Kara." Lizzie introduced herself and held out her hand to Derrick.

Derrick smiled and shook her hand. "Derrick Halson."

"Nice to meet you." Lizzie smiled. "How can I help?"

They spent the next hour going through the building records and pulling out blueprints. Once Kara had copies of the plans for her father's house, the two projects they needed to get for Johnny, and a set of her own house, they were ready to leave.

"Give me your number. What are you doing this weekend? We HAVE to hang out," Kara said to Lizzie when she and Derrick were getting ready to leave.

Lizzie laughed, and they exchanged numbers. After a quick text to make sure things were entered correctly, they set up tentative plans for lunch on Saturday.

"Well look at you," Derrick chuckled when they reached the bike again, "running into people and not even being upset about it."

Kara shot him a bright smile and shrugged. "Lizzie was one of my best friends at my private school. She was one of the normal, down-to-earth rich kids."

"Is there such a thing?" Derrick asked, raising an eyebrow.

"You just met one of the few exceptions." Kara smiled fondly.

Derrick nodded and climbed on the bike. "Come on, baby girl. I'm starving." He shot her a wink.

Feeling lighter than she had in a long time, Kara climbed on behind him and leaned in, ready to enjoy the night.

Chapter Eighteen

WHEN THEY GOT HOME, Kara was still flying on cloud nine from her encounter with Lizzie. She bounced into the house and right into Johnny's arms with a smile on her face.

"What's got you so excited?" he asked as he slid his hands around her hips and laced his fingers together at her lower back. He pulled her body flush against his and stared down at her with those sinful deep blue eyes.

He was still dressed in a black work shirt and sawdust was sprinkled over him. He had on a backward black baseball, and his blond beard was trimmed shorter than usual, not so scruffy but still enough to run her fingers through. He looked fantastic, as all her men always did, but the pregnancy hormones were definitely amping up as she stared up at him with her heart racing.

"You are a brilliant man, Johnathan Taylor," she told him and rose up on her tippy-toes to press a kiss to his lips.

He chuckled lightly as he kissed her back. "Well, we already knew that. But what really has you so happy?"

"You needed blueprints, and it made me think about my father's house. So we got the blueprints for there too," she told him.

Shock widened his eyes. "Fuck yes!" he exclaimed and picked her up in a bear hug. "Quick thinking, Princess. I fucking love that about you."

She laughed and kissed him again as he spun her around. "Where's Kevin?" she asked when they pulled apart.

"In the shower," Johnny answered and set her back on her feet.

Kara smiled and slid onto a barstool at the kitchen island. "What's for dinner?" she asked, looking at the stove where Johnny had clearly been cooking before they came home.

"Pork chops," Johnny replied and moved toward the stove. "Anything else happen today?"

"I ran into an old friend from high school. Lizzie. I haven't seen her since we both left for college," Kara told him. Then she launched into their plan for lunch on Saturday.

Johnny listened as she rambled on, a smile on his face while he stirred veggies on the stove. Once the food was under control, he walked around the island and wrapped his arms around her again.

He stood behind her, his front pressed to her back, pulling her tight against him. "I'm glad you're happy, Princess."

Kara smiled and soaked up his warmth. "Me too. I've been stressing too much lately," she quietly admitted.

Johnny rubbed her arms and pressed a kiss to the crown of her head. "I love you."

"I love you too." She sighed and reached up to squeeze his forearms.

Johnny and the boys had spent the evening poring over the blueprints for her father's house. In the end, they found exactly what they were looking for: several rooms were on the blueprints that were not visible or noticeable while in the house.

Kara made a call to District Attorney Lacey Winters. They would need a search warrant to enter the house if they wanted anything they found to hold up in court. Lacey promised she would get her that warrant.

By nine the following morning, they had the warrant. So, bright and early, they let themselves into her father's house armed with sledgehammers and pry bars—and a team of police officers—and got to work. There were three hidden rooms shown on the blueprints, but there were also a couple questionable areas that the boys wanted to check, places where there was lots of dead space listed on the drawing but where something could possibly be hidden.

Kara mostly stood back and watched her sexy men demo her father's house. Heavy sledgehammers swung and drywall shattered, large gaping holes being left behind. For every wall they opened, Kara grew more agitated when they didn't find anything.

Well, they did find things—small safes full of jewels and guns, a shit ton of guns—but they didn't find documents or ways to open the three very large vaults they found.

Kara sighed and looked around at the mess they had made. Chunks of drywall littered the floor; dust covered everything, including her guys. Sweat made their shirts cling to them like second skin. She couldn't help but stare at the three of them as their muscles bulged and sweat glistened on tattooed skin. They were hotter than fire.

Derrick smirked at her. He had just lifted the hem of his shirt to wipe the sweat from his face when he caught her staring at his abs.

She loved that her men were so toned and fit.

"What's on your mind, baby girl?" Derrick asked, his voice dropping an octave.

Kara let her gaze roam lazily over his sweaty body before she met his sparkling green eyes. A smug grin greeted her, and she smiled lazily. "Just enjoying the view."

Derrick laughed. "I'm sure you are, baby girl."

"You guys know how to get into those vaults?" Kara asked, changing the subject.

"I already called Jack," Kevin said, lifting his shoulder to wipe his face on his sleeve. "He knows a guy. They'll be here soon."

Kara smiled at Kevin. He was always thinking of what she needed before she even thought to ask for it; all her men were. "Thank you." She moved closer and pressed a quick kiss to his lips. He was dirty and sweaty.

He smirked, as if reading her thoughts. "What, don't want to get dirty?"

She wrinkled her nose and stepped away from him.

"Not what you usually say, Princess," Johnny said from behind her.

She rolled her eyes and turned toward him. "Usually you boys have a better way of getting me dirty." She grinned.

"That can be arr—"

"Knock, knock," a male voice called out.

Kara startled and looked toward the door. Jack Adams, Kevin's brother, stood at the end of the hallway with a bright smile on his face. A little younger and leaner than his brother but still very much as attractive, with the same black hair and brown eyes as Kevin, there was no mistaking they were related. He had a mischievous air about him and the smirk to match.

"Hey Jack." Kara beamed and moved toward him.

Jack met her halfway and pulled her into a hug. "Kara, as beautiful as ever," Jack greeted.

"Still a charmer, I see." She smiled and hugged him back.

"Adams family trait," Jack joked as he pulled away.

Kara gave him a smile and turned to face his friend. He looked familiar, large and intimidating. He was dressed in a pressed suit with hints of tattoos peeking over his collar. "I've seen you before," Kara said as she took him in.

He gave her a tight smile. "Noah Jameson. I own Jameson Security, a private security firm. You saw me guarding Miss Stonewall from afar that day in the bar."

Understanding dawned, and Kara nodded. "Kara Carmichael," she introduced, shaking his hand. "How is Stephanie? I'm afraid it's been a while since I've spoken to her" Kara frowned, realizing just how long it had been since she had talked to her friend. She didn't mean for it to be so long, but life had gotten in the way.

Noah gave her another tight smile. "She could use a friend."

Kara nodded. "I'll give her a call," she promised and looked around at the group of men. "These are my guys." She motioned toward Kevin, Johnny, and Derrick. "Boys, introduce yourselves. I've got a phone call to make."

There was a rumble of laughter behind her, but she didn't stay to listen. Instead, she headed for the stairs, searching for a quiet part of her father's mansion.

Kara gave Stephanie a call only to learn her friend was not doing well. She was stressing out over a job that she wouldn't or couldn't tell Kara about. But she had nothing but good things to say about Noah Jameson and his impressive suit.

"So how far down do those tattoos go?" Kara goaded, a smile on her face. She paced her father's bedroom while she spoke on the phone.

Stephanie laughed lightly. "I wouldn't know. He's been extremely professional, even when I was having hissy fits over constantly being followed." Stephanie sighed heavily.

Kara could read between the lines. She may not know her friend as well as she used to, but she could still tell when she was freaking the fuck out. "How often is he following you?" Kara asked.

"Noah and his team have moved in. There's four of them," Stephanie grumbled. "Four extremely large, tattooed meatheads. They've taken over my house. They constantly smell like sweat and too much cologne and *fucking man*."

The laugh exploded out of Kara before she could stifle it. She loved when Stephanie got all riled up, the times she spoke her mind and didn't always have tact. She was funny that way. "I'm sorry girl; I don't mean to laugh." She chuckled.

"Yes, you do." Stephanie sighed and chuckled slightly herself. "I know I'm being ridiculous."

"No." Kara immediately sobered. "You're not being ridiculous. Never. It was just your delivery. You have every right to your feelings, especially if they've invaded your home. You probably have no privacy."

"Zilch. Zero privacy. Except maybe in the shower. Even then, I wouldn't put it past them to be listening at the door." Stephanie groaned.

Kara felt bad for her friend. "What's the threat about?"

Stephanie sighed. "It's a job I took a while back—it's come back to bite me in the ass. I can't really talk about it, but I was receiving threats, hence the need for private security."

Kara frowned. "Threats enough to have four full-time guards move in?"

"Yeah." Stephanie sighed. "It's not as bad as it sounds. Most of the time they're great..."

"But?" Kara prompted, knowing her friend sometimes needed a little push to share her feelings when she got bashful.

"But," Stephanie's voice lowered dramatically, "I'm so sexually frustrated," she admitted. "They walk around shirtless and sweaty after workouts, all bulging muscles and thick thighs." She groaned.

Kara laughed heartily. "So, why haven't you jumped one of them yet?"

Stephanie sighed.

Kara could practically see her shy friend fidgeting at the thought of making the first move. "Turnabout is fair play," Kara pointed out. "You wear those tight spandex outfits when you work out: sports bra and short shorts. Walk around in those longer after you work out, do yoga in the living room, change your clothes with the door open but have sexy lingerie on," Kara suggested.

"Hmm," Stephanie hummed thoughtfully. "I like some of that." She chuckled darkly.

Kara laughed. "Noah seems…" Kara waited to see if her friend would pick up the thought thread.

"Girl, he's so fucking hot and sweet. He's too fucking professional, though. The way he looks at me," she gave another dramatic sigh, "it fucking burns me," she admitted.

Kara fanned herself. "Hot damn, woman."

Stephanie laughed softly. "I don't know, Kara. I've had relationships over the years…but no one has ever made me feel the way the four of them do. I couldn't choose just one of them."

"Who says you have to?" Kara shot back immediately.

Stephanie let out a soft sigh. "I don't think I'm brave enough for that."

"You know, Steph, I think you might just surprise yourself," Kara said slowly, knowing she had to walk a fine line with her friend. Stephanie was softer than Kara in a lot of ways. She didn't have the hardened shell that Kara had. She hid behind her numbers and let the world pass her by.

"Thanks Kara. You're a great friend."

Kara smiled sadly. "I wish I could be a better friend now when it sounds like you need it. I'm afraid I won't be able to get away until this shit with my father blows over."

"Girl, I get it. I'm swamped myself. Funny how life does that." Stephanie chuckled wryly.

"Tell me about it." Kara groaned. "Alright girl, I gotta let you go. We've been tearing into my father's house, pulling out his hidden safes. Jack said that Noah could get into any safe, so hopefully they've made progress by now."

"Good luck, girl, and thanks for calling. I'll take your guidance under advisement." Stephanie chuckled.

Kara laughed. "Do it. Report back."

"Love you, Kara." Stephanie laughed.

"Love you too, Steph. It'll get better, I promise," Kara told her before she hung up the phone. She laughed softly as she walked out of her father's room. Who would have thought her prim and proper college roommate would be entertaining the idea of four guys?

Kara headed back down to the basement, where she found her three men, plus Jack and Noah, examining the contents of the open vault. "You got in?" Kara exclaimed with a smile.

"Yes ma'am," Noah answered, looking up from the vault he was working on.

"Anything?" Kara asked her boys, walking over to the table they were congregated around. They were sifting through papers.

"We've found deeds for properties all over the world," Kevin admitted. "Haven't found anything in the Caribbean."

"Yet," Derrick added. "Haven't found it yet," he clarified. "This is only one vault. There's two more."

Kara sighed and nodded. It was going to be a long day.

"Jackpot!" Derrick yelled from down the hall.

Kara perked up from her spot on the couch. After it was clear they weren't easily going to find what they were looking for, she had gone to sit down and read a book. The loitering police officers were annoying her, and watching her men get dirty was only turning her on, so she found a quiet place to cool down.

"Jackpot, baby girl," Derrick shouted again, running into the living room.

She grinned and jumped up from the couch. "For real this time?"

"Oh yeah," Kevin said enthusiastically as he walked in carrying a stack of papers. "Location of the law firm in the Caymans. His condo. A house. Some other businesses there," Kevin said. "His banking info."

"Fuck yes." Kara cheered as she looked over the stack of documents Kevin handed her. "Jack," Kara said, as she stared down at everything.

"Yes, ma'am," Jack answered, the smile evident in his voice as he walked over to her.

"Can you freeze his accounts?" She kept her voice low and looked up at him, hopeful.

Jack paused midstep, the smile sliding off his face. "Theoretically? Maybe. It's highly illegal. I'd have to hack into his bank."

Kara frowned. "Can you at least track his most recent movements? We need to make sure he's there, and I'll call Winters about the accounts."

"I can do that," Jack agreed as Noah stepped into the living room behind him.

Kara turned to Johnny and reached out for him. He stepped toward her and grasped her hands with his. "You have to promise me," she said slowly, keeping her voice down as she glanced at Kevin and Derrick also. "Promise me," she stressed, "that you'll bring him home *alive*."

Johnny squeezed her fingers. "I can't promise you that," he answered, his voice low so they wouldn't be overheard by the officers in the other room.

"*Johnny*," she stressed quietly, squeezing his fingers tighter. "You don't understand. The *only* way I get control of Carmichael and

Associates is if he goes down for murder. I can't claim the firm, his assets, any of it, without him being alive and sentenced to prison."

Johnny scowled, looking down at her.

"Please Johnny," she begged. She stepped toward him and let go of his fingers, pushing his hands away so she could step into his body. She cupped the back of his neck and pulled his face down to meet hers. "I *need* him alive."

Johnny's hands gripped her hips. He rested his forehead against hers. "He tried to kill you," Johnny said softly.

Kara nodded slowly, rubbing her hand over his cheek. "I know," she murmured. "I also know that the best way to actually *hurt* my father is to take everything he spent his life building and make it *mine*, to give it legally to the child he never truly wanted."

Johnny let out a low growl, his voice gravelly when he finally spoke. "OK, Princess. I promise I won't kill him." He pulled away and pressed a kiss to her forehead before he stepped back.

Kara turned to Kevin and Derrick. Both of them were staring at her with similar expressions of annoyance and disappointment. "Please," she asked, her eyes darting between the two of them.

Kevin's shoulders were tense beneath his leather cut. His dark chocolate eyes narrowed on her. "Do you even want what he built?" Kevin asked.

Kara nodded. "I might not give a shit about the money or the properties, but I love what I do. I love being managing partner of

Carmichael and Associates. I love the people I work with daily. I want that."

Kevin smiled softly and moved toward her. He wrapped her in his arms and lowered his forehead to hers. "I know you do. I love seeing you so happy when you walk the halls of that building. Everyone loves and respects you. I want you to have that. If putting him behind bars is the only way, then I promise I won't kill your father."

She smiled and pressed a kiss to his lips.

They pulled apart a moment later, and Kara turned to Derrick. He was standing a few feet away, with his arms crossed over his chest. His disappointment had morphed into anger, and she didn't know how to proceed. Derrick was the jokester and laid back—he wasn't the hothead, but Devil could be—and she didn't usually deal with Devil.

She walked over to him and waited. "You going to make me beg?" she asked him.

"Is that an option?" he asked.

"I won't get on my knees for this, Derrick." She shook her head. This was not the time, and she wasn't in the mood for power plays. This was life and death, and her fucking livelihood was at stake. She needed this to all be aboveboard, as much as it could be.

"I didn't think you would." Derrick dropped his arms and shook his head. "I love you, baby girl. I love you and our unborn child," he said, placing a hand on her flat belly.

There was a soft gasp from behind them. She assumed it was Jack, because Kevin quickly moved away—they hadn't told family yet, besides Marcos and the clubs.

"I just want you safe. Your father already tried to kill you once. He almost succeeded too." Derrick sighed and slid his hand from her belly to her waist. He pulled her against him as his other hand came up and cradled her face.

Kara wrapped her arms around his neck and leaned into him. She didn't even mind how dusty and sweaty he was. "I know, and I was able to protect myself," she said softly. "Please Derrick. I need him sentenced for murder for the board to officially make me CEO."

Derrick sighed heavily. "I hate him."

Kara pressed a kiss to his lips. "Me too."

"Alright, baby girl. I'm gonna beat him to holy hell, though," Derrick conceded.

"Fine." Kara smirked and pressed another kiss to his lips.

"That's an option?" Johnny asked from behind her.

Kara laughed softly. "Not too badly. I need him to be able to appear unharmed on arrival."

"Nothing visible. Got it," Derrick shot back with a smirk.

Kara rolled her eyes and pulled away from him. "If we're done here, let's go home."

A throat cleared behind her, and Kara turned to see Noah Jameson standing in the doorway. "If it's cool, I'm gonna head out. I opened all the safes for you."

Kara beamed and headed toward him. "Thank you so much, Noah. Seriously. I appreciate it," Kara gushed, stopping before him. "You were a lifesaver today."

Noah gave her an easy smile. "Anytime. Things around here are fun." He chuckled.

Kara laughed and stepped toward him, opening her arms. Noah leaned down and gave her a friendly hug. "It was nice to meet you," she said as she let him go.

"You too," Noah said.

"I told Steph, when things calm down here...and there, we'll have to get together."

A dark look passed across Noah's eyes, but he blinked it away quickly. He plastered a smile on his face as he nodded. "Sounds great."

Jack and Kevin escorted him out of the house as Kara turned to Johnny and Derrick. "Something's going on with Stephanie. I'm worried about her."

"I think Jameson and his team have her completely guarded," Johnny said. "We were talking to him about his life in the military. He's ex–Special Forces, ran in some of the same circles we did." Johnny motioned between him and Derrick. "I think they have it handled."

Kara frowned and leaned into his arms. "I hope you're right," she murmured.

"I hope you're right about your father and the board," Johnny countered.

"Me too." Kara sighed.

Chapter Nineteen

I T HAD BEEN A long time since Kara had stayed late at the office. Before her attack, before she started dating her boys, she had been a workaholic. Most days she started early and left well after eight or nine p.m., especially in the lead-up to a trial. She needed her ducks all in a row and her case airtight.

She might not be leading the case against her father, but she was assisting Winters with anything she could. That meant gathering even more evidence. She had handed over access to her storage facility already, and Winters' team, along with Danvers, was neck deep in boxes.

The additional information Stephanie Stonewall had provided regarding the senior partners was what really had driven the indictment. Winters hadn't just gone after her father; she'd gone after several senior partners as well, Ken Laraway among them.

While they had all been indicted, only Laraway and her father had disappeared before they could be arrested. They were in the wind and on the run, so to speak. Winters was hoping their disappearances would put more pressure on the other indicted senior partners to talk.

Kara was growing more anxious the longer they went unapprehended. Her boys didn't want her going anywhere alone. She understood their reasoning, appreciated that they cared so much about her safety, but they were driving her crazy.

It had been two months since they were indicted and took off. Two months of her boys hovering constantly whenever they left the house. The only time they weren't up her ass was at home, the clubhouse, or the Carmichael and Associates building.

It had been months of no leads on where her father might be, months of digging through files and compiling the evidence that her father was a crooked lawyer, and months of putting up with Danvers' constant phone calls.

She was done with it all, over it completely. But she couldn't quit, not when they were so close, so she did what she always did when things got hard: she threw herself into her work, hence her need to work late. She was missing something, something key and vital to the case. Some little piece that would spell out just *where* her father and Laraway had gone and give some hints as to their next moves.

They had gained a wealth of information in the handful of safes Noah had cracked at her father's mansion but nothing truly *concrete* on his location, not without boots on the ground.

Her boys had left for the Cayman Islands the following afternoon. That had been a week ago. Jack had given them his private jet to use. Kara didn't want to risk using her father's and having it get back to him. She had hoped they'd be back by now, that she'd have answers.

Her boys had been scouring every property and address they knew about in order to bring her father to justice. They were coming up empty-handed, hitting brick wall after brick wall.

Vince had had forty years to plan his exit and cover his tracks. He was a billionaire with properties all over the world and his own private plane. It could be months before Johnny, Derrick, and Kevin found him.

In the meantime, Jack had tapped into her father's security systems, his bank accounts, and his credit cards. There wasn't a move Vince could make that Jack wouldn't know about.

But they still hadn't been able to find him.

Kara sighed in frustration as she placed yet another box of files onto the stack she had already sorted through. Ten. There were ten boxes stacked there that she had looked through just that day alone, not to mention the million other ones she'd combed in the last month. Two months. Three months. It was exhausting.

The lights dimmed beyond her open office door.

She frowned and glanced at the clock. It was only eight p.m.; the lights weren't scheduled to start dimming until after ten.

In the office remodel Taylor Construction had completed while she was out with her injuries, they'd removed the glass walls and installed drywall instead—the idea had been to allow for privacy and confidentiality when meeting with clients.

Now Kara was cursing that thought process. She'd love to be able to look out and see if anyone was in the waiting area outside her office without alerting them to her presence.

She grabbed her phone and slipped it into her garter belt, at the small of her back, beneath her pencil skirt. She hoped that it would go unnoticed in the event of an abduction. She tiptoed toward the door, wondering if she was being a paranoid idiot.

She had fought tooth and nail with Johnny and the guys regarding staying late at work without them. She had claimed that the building had security and that several people stayed late every night, that she wouldn't be alone in the building. And there usually were most nights, hence her wondering if she was being paranoid.

Before she could make it to her office door, four armed assailants stormed in. They were dressed head to toe in black, including the ski masks they had pulled over their faces. Assault rifles were strapped to their bodies and trained on her.

Kara froze, blood rushing to her ears as her heart hammered in her chest. She tried to focus on the four men in front of her but couldn't hear them above the yelling.

She soon realized it was the first man in front of her who was yelling. "Get down! On your knees!"

She failed to comply, failed to process his words.

There was a sharp prick in her neck before things went dark.

Her last thought was of her unborn baby.

Drip.

Drip.

Drip.

Kara blinked open her eyes as nausea rolled in her belly. She was cold, so cold. The thin, bare mattress she was sprawled on offered little insulation against the cold seeping through the concrete floor beneath it.

Her body and head ached. Her clothes were damp. The cold was in her bones.

Kara groaned softly and turned her head to find the source of the incessant dripping noise. She froze when she saw the man seated in an orange plastic chair like something out of a hospital waiting room. He was leaning back, his ankles crossed above his heavy boots. His muscular arms covered a paunchy belly. Dark eyes stared at her from sunken sockets.

There was a deadly air about him, as if he were more dead inside than alive. Or at least that was how his eyes portrayed his inner thoughts.

"Who are you?" Kara asked softly, forcing herself to get answers before her untimely death.

The man stared at her. He didn't answer her, didn't move, just stared.

Kara looked around the room, trying to get her bearings. There wasn't much to see, though. It was a ten-by-ten concrete room with a lone light bulb hanging from a chain in the center of the room. A conduit ran along the ceiling toward the door before it turned and went straight up through the concrete ceiling.

There was a camera in the corner of the room, above her captor, and there was a bucket in the opposite side of the room, which she assumed was supposed to be her bathroom facility. Besides the threadbare mattress in the corner and the orange hospital chair in the opposite corner...there wasn't anything else in the cell.

Except for Kara and the man watching her.

Kara sat up slowly, keeping her eyes on her captor.

When he didn't move, she shimmied her body backward into the corner of the room and brought her knees up to her chest. She wrapped her arms around her legs and tried to warm herself.

The man in front of her didn't move, but he also never stopped watching her with his unblinking black, almost dead eyes. It was unnerving.

Kara looked above him to the blinking red light of the security camera. She stared into the camera instead of the dead eyes of her captor.

Kara didn't stare at the camera for long before there was a beep outside the door, a lock clicked loudly as it disengaged, and the door swung open.

Two armed guards, dressed in black from the neck down, stood in the doorway. Both had thick shoulders and were well built; both were of Hispanic descent. The miliary style clothing threw her off. She didn't know of any gangs that had this kind of operation.

"*Vamos*," the man on the right barked.

Kara slowly uncurled her body. She wondered if she should pretend to not understand Spanish. She also wondered where they were taking her and if she was about to die—the thought sent a spike of fear through her heart.

She was wobbly as she got to her feet. She steeled her spine and pushed back her shoulders. If she was going to her death, she wasn't going to cower in fear.

Her legs were weak as she walked toward the guards.

One of them moved forward and roughly grabbed her wrist, yanking her forward. She stumbled and fell into him. She used her momentum to her advantage and brought her knee up and got him right in the balls.

He grunted and curled up.

Kara couldn't even turn to the other guard before a hand wrapped around her neck and shoved her against the wall, hard. Her head snapped back against the concrete wall, her ears ringing as spots dotted her vision.

The man towered over her, his hand squeezing tighter. "Fucking *cunt*," he ground out.

Kara gasped for breath.

"I'm going to enjoy breaking you." He growled in her face, squeezing her neck tighter.

Her vision dimmed. She tried to lift her hand and claw at his hand, but her movements were slow, jerky.

He abruptly let go, and she collapsed to the concrete floor in a heap. Her knees screamed in pain as they smacked the hard floor. Her chest was heaving as she drew in gasping breaths.

Both guards left, and the door locked back into place.

Kara was still on the floor when the man in the orange chair shifted and stood up. She froze, having forgotten about him. She looked up and found his dead eyes on her once again. Always staring.

"Hora de despertar, muñeca" (time to get up, Poppet). His voice was deep and lilting, almost singsongy. It was creepy.

Kara didn't move. She didn't know how much they knew about her, but she decided not to give away that she spoke Spanish fluently. She didn't know if she was being foolish or if it would grant her a level of immunity, but it was all she had in the moment.

When she didn't respond or move, Paunchy stepped toward her and lowered a hand. He left his hand outstretched in front of her face and waited.

She tensed, not expecting kindness from him at all, not from Mr. Dead Eyes. She must have already been losing her mind, she thought, as her brain created different names for a man whose true name she didn't know.

Taking a risk, because she needed an ally if she wanted to get out of this prison alive, Kara placed her hand—and her trust—into that of the dead-eyed man before her.

His hand was rough and calloused, as she'd expected, but it was warm and gentle as he pulled her to her feet.

Her knees ached from her fall, but she stared at her captor unflinchingly.

He nudged her with her hand back toward the mattress. When she stepped forward, he dropped her hand and returned to his chair.

Kara frowned slightly as she moved toward the bed and slowly lowered herself back down. The cold, damp air was seeping into her joints, and she wished she had at least a blanket to cover up with. She was still in her work clothes, and the silky green blouse and pencil skirt did little to block the chill.

She curled back up at the top of the mattress, keeping her back pressed into the corner.

Chapter Twenty

"She's not answering her phone," Kevin snapped from the front seat of the work van they had rented to do the snatch and grab of Vince Carmichael and Ken Laraway.

Johnny glared at the two men he had bound and gagged on the floor of the utility van. "Call her again," he ordered.

Ken let out a laugh from behind his gag.

Ice chilled Johnny's spine. He leaned forward and ripped the gag from Laraway's mouth. "Where is she?" Johnny growled.

Laraway laughed again. "You'll never find her."

Johnny snapped out a punch so quick Laraway didn't know what hit him. Devil stomped on Laraway's rib cage with a heavy boot. There was an audible crunch beneath his boot before Laraway screamed like a little bitch.

"Where the FUCK is she?" Johnny roared. He glanced at Devil across the enclosed space.

Laraway laughed in response.

Devil shook his head grimly.

Johnny leaned over and decked Laraway hard enough to knock him out. His body fell limply to the side, hitting the floor with a thud.

Vince refused to meet anyone's stare. He kept his gaze down as he glared at the zip ties Johnny had slapped on his wrists—fastened so tightly they cut into his wrists.

"Marcos." Kevin spoke up from the front. Johnny looked over to see him driving the van, a cell phone pressed to his ear. "We think Kara's been kidnapped. She's not answering her phone. Laraway indicated he's behind it." Kevin was quiet for a moment, listening. "Search it anyway; we've got them both. We'll be flying out soon." He hung up the phone and met Johnny's gaze in the rearview mirror. "Kara kicked him out of her office. He said she's been working late all week. He's going in to search."

"MOTHERFUCKER!" Johnny spat out, his blood boiling. He reached for his phone and dialed Kara himself.

Johnny paced the cabin of Jack's private plane like a caged lion. He hated flying, hated the tin can in the sky. He felt locked up, itchy. Not to mention, he was pissed the fuck off.

Laraway was still unconscious from the punch in the van. They had immediately rushed for the airport, knowing they were breaking half a dozen international laws. They managed to play off half carrying Laraway onboard by acting like he was drunk. They immediately dumped him in the bedroom and hog-tied his ass in bed.

Vince Carmichael, on the other hand, stoically moved where they put him and kept his mouth shut after they pulled off his gag. He was now sitting in a cabin chair, dozing against the window.

Or he appeared to be dozing.

Johnny didn't care.

"We need a plan." Kevin sighed, rubbing a hand over the back of his neck.

Johnny shot a look at Carmichael. The man's chest was rising and falling steadily. He didn't trust that he wasn't faking it. "We'll move them to a safe house when we land. We need information. If Kara really is missing, they might be the only way to find her."

"Fucking bullshit." Devil swore and stood up. He started pacing at the other end of the rather spacious yet still-too-small jet.

Kevin leaned forward in his chair and rested his elbows on his knees. He slid a hand from the back of his neck over his head slowly and repeatedly, as if breaking up the tension that had settled there.

Johnny knew that move—it was one of the few tells his best friend had. As stress settled onto Kevin's shoulders, he let out a slow breath before he rubbed his eyes. "We need a plan," he said again, his voice low.

"We'll take them back to the compound, interrogate them. We'll find her," Johnny answered, giving his friend a solid plan.

"No," Kevin said, slowly unfurling from the chair. He stood and faced Johnny head-on. "No club. This stays among the three of us."

Johnny frowned, eyeing his brother. Very rarely did Kevin ever question Johnny's decisions. "We'll need the club's help rescuing Kara if she's been taken," Johnny shot back.

"If she's been taken, we'll ask for help," Kevin conceded.

"He's right," Derrick jumped in. "This is personal. We take them somewhere else, interrogate them ourselves, then turn them over to the DA."

Johnny stared at his two best friends, his brothers, men he would die for, kill for. "Alright." He nodded slowly, thinking quickly. "We can take them to my dad's house; the basement has a holding cell."

Both men nodded, and slowly the three of them returned to their seats and settled in for the rest of the flight.

When they landed, Kevin placed a call to Jack, who informed them of a vehicle waiting for them on the tarmac. As they climbed down the plane stairs, the driver got out and walked around the front of the Suburban.

"Jameson." Johnny paused when he saw Noah walking his way. The man was in another impeccable suit, navy blue this time. He looked like he was headed to a board meeting, not about to be illegally transporting two bound prisoners.

"Taylor," Noah greeted and shook Johnny's hand. "Jack said you found the bastards?"

Johnny smirked. "Sure did. Gonna find out what they know before we turn 'em over. You got a problem with that?" he questioned, already knowing the man's answer.

"I'd help you kill 'em if that's what the missus wanted," he vowed, completely serious.

Johnny nodded and slapped him on the shoulder. "Appreciate that. If only I could convince her," he grumbled.

Noah nodded, and both men turned to see Derrick and Kevin march Carmichael and a now conscious Laraway down the stairs.

Johnny headed over to help, and Noah got back behind the wheel to make a fast getaway.

Laraway grumbled through his gag, but Carmichael was utterly silent.

Johnny stared at the fucker, wondering if the man was just that calm, cool, and collected. Is that where Kara got it from? Or was the man in a state of shock, dazed and confused?

They wouldn't know until they started laying into the men.

Good thing Johnny and his boys were good at getting answers.

And today, they had just a little more motivation.

Chapter Twenty-One

K ARA SHIFTED IN HER corner. Mr. Dead Eyes was still watching her. She had to pee, and she was shivering steadily. The cold was unrelenting. She wanted to go home. She wanted Johnny, and Kevin, and Derrick. She wanted to be wrapped in their arms and held tight, needed the safety and security they gave her.

She wanted her brother too. Fucking Marcos and his stupid overbearing nature—she would do anything to listen to him snip at her now.

Most of all, she wanted Mr. Dead Eyes to STOP. FUCKING. STARING.

His unblinking stares were unnerving.

Was this some kind of psychological warfare? Were they trying to dehumanize her? What was the point of this? Who were these people?

She slammed her eyes closed as she felt tears starting to well. She forced herself to do her therapy breathing. Her structured breathing...that she hadn't had to practice as often since she started dating her guys. Her mind flashed back to that day with Derrick in the basement of Carmichael and Associates when he caught her in the middle of a panic attack and how he hadn't even questioned her as he calmed her with his presence.

Her anxiety attacks had been few and far between since her guys came into her life. Even when she and Johnny were at each other's throats, he was still a source of calm and security for her. Now she only felt any kind of overwhelming anxiety when life was out of her control.

The thought only made her panic rise further.

She kept her eyes closed and focused on her breathing. Breathe in for four seconds and hold for seven seconds, then slowly release the breath for eight seconds.

Breathe in for four seconds.

Hold for seven.

Release for eight.

Breathe in four.

Hold for seven.

Release for eight.

~*~

She must have dozed off or fallen into a meditative state, because when she came to, she was still tucked into the corner with her knees against her chest, but her head was resting on her knees and her body felt cramped, like she had stayed in the position for too long.

The lights in the room were off, plunging the room into complete darkness. The small blinking red light of the security camera was the only source of light.

Kara froze. She wasn't alone.

Was Mr. Dead Eyes *still* sitting in that chair?

Fucking hell. She didn't know what to do. Her bladder was *screaming* at her. She needed to go. She did NOT want to go in front of him...but in the dark? Could she manage that? She didn't have a choice; the pain was unbearable.

She vaguely remembered the location of the bucket in the corner. She slowly unfurled her body and inched off the bed. When there was no movement from the staring man in the corner, she made her way to the bucket and quickly unzipped her pencil skirt.

She put her back to her captor and the camera and was quick about emptying her bladder, hoping she didn't give them too much of a show. She wouldn't put it past them to have a night vision camera mounted in there.

She breathed a sigh of relief when she finally finished, her body no longer in pain. She mentally wished for toilet paper, but drip-dried the best she could. When she was done and her clothes were back in place, she went back to her mattress and lay down, stretching out and giving her aching body a reprieve.

She was still cold, shivering slightly. She closed her eyes and focused on her breathing again.

She needed to survive this. Her baby needed her, and she would not let anything happen to her unborn child. She needed him or her as much as they would need her.

It was still dark when she woke again, and she felt the eyes on her immediately.

Staring. Unblinking.

The steady breathing of her captor was the only sound in the room. She saw only the blinking red light from the camera.

And always she had the burning feeling of being watched.

Fear welled inside her again. This was their plan, to slowly drive her crazy. Psychological warfare of the most basic kind. Her chest shuddered with a muffled sob. She squeezed her eyes shut and started breathing.

Four seconds in. Seven seconds hold. Eight seconds release.

Repeat.

Kara was roused roughly from sleep as hands grabbed her ankles and yanked her down the mattress. She screamed and kicked reflexively, managing to kick the man in the face. When she realized what was happening, she kicked out more frantically.

There was a black-clad guard looming over her. The ski mask covered his face, leaving nothing but a sliver for his dark eyes to peer out. "Come here, you little bitch," the man growled, his voice deep.

"Fuck off," she shouted and aimed another kick at his head.

His hand snapped out and grabbed her ankle roughly. He twisted it and she was wrenched over, onto her belly. She scrambled on the mattress, trying to get away, when suddenly a fist swung out and caught her in the rib cage.

She cried out and went limp as something crunched and pain radiated out from her previously broken ribs. Overwhelming fear overtook her as she instinctively curled into a ball to protect her belly and unborn child. "Please, don't." She gasped. "I'm pregnant," she admitted, feeling like she was giving up a piece of her soul. She only hoped she could reach some human side of him and gain some mercy from the guard.

The man paused and glared down at her.

She gasped, trying to catch her breath. Her chest ached. She was sure he rebroke the same ribs and could only hope one wouldn't puncture her lung again.

Surprise washed over her as the guard stood up and backed away.

She closed her eyes and waited, resigned to her fate.

The door slammed shut a moment later, and Kara finally opened her eyes. The guard was gone, and she was once again alone with Mr. Dead Eyes.

His eyes were on her, as they always were, his expression unchanged. She wasn't sure why she thought her admission would affect him. He was a stone wall and Dead Eyes.

Kara closed her eyes and went back to her breathing. It was harder now that her ribs were on fire. She focused anyway. She needed to stay calm and make a plan. She needed to get out of this place.

THE BASEMENT IN MAC Taylor's house was nothing to write home about—simple and unfinished. Bare light bulbs hung from the rafters; a couple LED strip lights gave more light when needed. It was mostly storage.

Johnny didn't even want to think about the memories hidden in those boxes. One day he'd have the energy to sort through them, but until then, he had business to attend to.

Vince Carmichael and Ken Laraway were strung up by their wrists from the ceiling in the center of the room. Johnny and the boys had to move stacks of boxes out of the way to make room and to protect the memorabilia from any potential blood splatter.

Carmichael was still as stoic as he'd been on the plane. A resigned sort of calm had settled over him. Johnny eyed the man warily. It wasn't what he'd expected from him.

At sixty-five, Vince Carmichael's blond hair had taken on a white blond sheen that was more gray than blond. His blue eyes had crinkled in the corners. He would have been attractive enough, if he weren't a spineless weasel.

The utter lack of fight from the man grated on Johnny's nerves. As if feeling Johnny's stare, Vince looked up and met his gaze. "You're an utter piece of shit," Johnny told him. "Do you even care that your daughter has been kidnapped? Do you even care what happens to her?"

"That moneygrubbing whore should have stayed in the ghetto where she came from," Laraway spat out. His body swayed slightly from the force of the words he spewed.

"That right?" Derrick drawled, circling around the hanging men so they could see him leering at them. "You feel the same, daddy dearest?"

Vince stayed quiet.

Johnny sneered. "You know, your daughter asked us to spare your life," Johnny told him, moving out of the shadows.

Vince's gaze finally met his.

"Still got nothing to say, Carmichael? Cat got your tongue?" Derrick taunted.

Kevin walked over too. "Why should he care? He hired someone to attack his own daughter."

"I had nothing to do with that." Vince finally spoke up.

"I don't believe you," Johnny shot back immediately.

Vince glared at him. "I may have told her to stop whoring herself out to the three of you, but I never had anyone attack her."

Ken laughed.

Johnny turned his head to look at the hanging rat. He crossed his arms over his chest. Laraway was the talker of the two; Johnny could wait for the man to spill his guts, or they'd make him. Either way, it wasn't any skin off his back.

"Where is she?" Devil asked Laraway, moving closer.

"You'll never find her," Laraway repeated.

Johnny rolled his eyes. "Strip him."

Devil pulled a knife from his belt and made quick work of slicing the ragged clothes from Laraway's paunchy body. Laraway thrashed against his bonds as Devil cut away his old button-up shirt and dress pants, leaving the man hanging in nothing but his briefs, his heavy belly hanging over his tighty-whities. It was a horrible image and would be burned into Johnny's skull for the rest of his days.

"He's been working with the snakes," Vince said.

"So have you, Carmichael. Don't put this all on him." Rockstar growled.

"I was working with Larry Buckley. I never spoke to the snakes or did business with them," Carmichael clarified.

"Because you pussied out in the end," Laraway snapped.

Vince rolled his eyes and turned away from the other man as much as he could while hanging from the ceiling.

"Devil, begin," Johnny ordered and leaned back against the wall.

"The snakes have a warehouse off of Route 9, out past old Sheppard's Mill," Vince said, eyeing Derrick warily.

Devil slid his Buck knife back into the sheath on his belt and walked over to a table against the wall, picking up a knife with an eight-inch blade. "One of you needs to start talking. Otherwise you're going to start losing limbs," Derrick drawled and started cleaning his fingernails with the tip of the blade.

Johnny would have rolled his eyes at his brother's dramatics if he weren't just as anxious to get this show on the road.

Devil leaned in and pressed the tip of the blade to Laraway's chest. The man screamed instantly, and Devil didn't let up. He slowly dragged the knife down Laraway's torso. When he thrashed too much for Devil to keep the cut straight, Rockstar moved in behind Laraway and held him steady.

Carmichael closed his eyes and tried to turn his head away.

Johnny walked over to the man and grabbed his jaw roughly. Vince's eyes snapped open as Johnny squeezed his face tightly and turned his head to look at his buddy. "You will watch this," Johnny threatened, his voice low, "because you will be next."

"I already told you where to find them!" Vince shouted. "They have a warehouse out past old Sheppard's Mill. If they have Kara, she's probably there!"

"Why?" Johnny growled, glaring at the man.

Vince tried to shake his head.

"Why?" Johnny growled again.

"She was never supposed to get hurt," Vince said.

"She was fucking attacked in her own home! She said your hit man Randall Diggins was the one to attack her," Johnny explained.

"I never sent Diggins after my daughter! I didn't have to—she'd already broken up with you three and walked away. She did what I told her, like she always does." Vince sneered. "I have total control over my daughter. I don't need to pay someone to beat the shit out of her."

Johnny growled and Laraway gasped in pain. "I paid Diggins. I wanted her dead," Laraway admitted.

"You bastard," Vince spat out.

"What else did you do, Kenny boy?" Devil crooned and dragged the knife down the other side of his chest.

"Told Las Serpientes they could do whatever they wanted with her." Laraway panted through the pain.

"Where is she?" Derrick asked.

"The warehouse. They have an elaborate warehouse there, high security. She'll be in the basement," Laraway said.

"Good boy," Derrick crooned before he sank the blade into Laraway's belly.

While Derrick went to work on Laraway, Johnny turned to Carmichael. "Now, Vincey boy, you're gonna listen while my brother disembowels your buddy here."

Vince squeezed his eyes shut. For an ex-military man, he'd sure gotten soft over the years.

Johnny laughed and pulled out his own blade. "What do you say, Vincey boy? Should we start in on you, or should we make a deal?"

"What do you want?" Vince breathed heavily.

Laraway screamed louder as Derrick really got to work on him. Blood splattered everywhere as Derrick stabbed Laraway in the thigh.

Johnny chuckled deeply. "I want to kill you," he admitted to Vince. "But your daughter asked me not to."

Vince heaved a heavy breath as a tear rolled down his cheek.

Johnny smirked. "I honestly don't know why she'd care. It's not like you ever gave a shit about her."

"That's not true," Vince snapped.

"Fine, you cared that she bent to your will and did whatever you told her," Johnny conceded. "Became your little puppet, someone you could flaunt to your friends. A perfect daughter that followed in your footsteps."

Vince shuddered as a sob overcame him. He looked utterly pathetic.

Johnny tsked ever so softly. "Kara might have asked me not to kill you, but what she doesn't know won't hurt her," Johnny taunted.

"No!" Vince cried. "Please. Please, don't kill me," he begged.

"And what are you going to do for me?" Johnny crooned.

"What do you want?" Vince asked immediately.

"A full confession," Johnny replied just as quickly. "Confess that you organized my father's death and had him framed for all those crimes, take the fall for all of it."

Laraway screamed again, and Johnny looked over to see Devil using his blade to pull out a loop of intestine. "Oh, that looks gruesome," Kevin commented offhandedly.

Vince sobbed violently and swayed in his chains. "OK!" he shouted.

"OK, what?" Johnny prompted.

"OK, I'll confess to having your father killed! I take sole blame." He complied. His eyes snapped open to meet Johnny's. "I'll tell them it was only me! I'll tell them how I framed your father and paid the serpents to kill him in jail, that I was behind all of it," Vince agreed.

Johnny smirked. "Good boy."

"Where's Laraway," Winters demanded as Johnny pulled up to the back of the police station, their designated meeting place.

Johnny put his truck in park and raised an eyebrow at the DA. "I brought you Carmichael. Who gives a shit about Laraway?" he asked.

"The case will be stronger with all of the accused standing trial," she replied, looking thoroughly annoyed.

Johnny threw open the van door and climbed out. "Well, I brought you fucking Carmichael on a silver fucking platter. See to it that he goes down for the murder of my father."

Several police officers swarmed the vehicle, and Johnny stepped out of the way. He watched as Carmichael was pulled from the back seat and an officer started reading him his rights.

Vince Carmichael didn't say a word the whole way into the precinct.

Winters followed after him, and Johnny shook his head. "You're welcome," he called after the surly DA.

"Thanks," she called over her shoulder absentmindedly.

Chapter Twenty-Three

T HE COOL NIGHT AIR pressed in around him. Autumn had officially arrived in northern Illinois as October settled in. It was just after eight, but it was as dark as midnight. Marcos rode through Creekton on his Harley, wondering where the fuck things had gone wrong.

His sister was missing.

Axel, Phoenix, and Blaze had been stationed outside her office building while Mayhem, Devil, and Rockstar were out of town searching for Carmichael.

Somehow the assailants had gotten the drop on Axel, taking him down while he stood guard outside the loading dock. They'd incapacitated him with a tranquillizer dart fired from a distance. He hadn't seen or heard anything.

When he didn't call in for the hourly check-in with Blaze and Phoenix, they had gone to investigate. They found him passed the fuck out on the ground. Immediately they had gone looking for Kara only to find the building empty.

They called Marcos immediately. He in turn called Johnny. As pissed as Johnny was, he said they had a guy that could pull up the camera footage and try and track Kara that way.

That had been almost twenty-four hours ago.

His skin itched every time he thought about how he'd failed his sister. She was his responsibility, had *always* been his responsibility, and he had failed her.

He couldn't afford to fail her again. He *had* to find her.

When Johnny called an hour ago with a location and told him to meet them there, Marcos didn't ask any questions and Johnny didn't elaborate.

Marcos turned the corner just past old Sheppard's Mill and saw his destination ahead. Stone and Dagger rode behind him, ready to go.

He slowed down as they neared what looked like an abandoned warehouse. Boarded up buildings sat empty in the middle of nowhere. What used to be a bustling meatpacking plant was now a decrepit bunch of buildings that not even one of those big-box-store distributors would want to buy.

This was the supposed hiding place of Las Serpientes, a fucking street gang that was notorious for its unyielding level of violence.

The Devil's Psychos had been at war with the gang off and on for years.

Buckley had garnered a tentative truce with the snakes in the last several years, but if they were responsible for Mac's death in County and his sister's kidnapping? War would be inevitable. He only hoped he could keep it out of Mourningside and away from his sister.

They killed their engines next to one of the furthest outbuildings and waited.

They had barely dismounted when headlights appeared in the distance. "You don't think it's a setup, do you?" Dagger asked.

"No," Marcos said, feeling confident in his truce with Johnny.

A moment later, a blacked-out cargo van rolled up beside them, and Johnny opened the driver's door.

"What do we know?" Marcos asked as the three of them climbed out of the van. His deep voice sounded loud in the now-silent night. They could only hope there were no cameras this far out from the warehouse that Johnny's surveillance team had scoped out.

"The big building in the middle has been fitted with a state-of-the-art security system; lots of upgrades have been made," Johnny said. "Our guy was able to hack in. She's there." Johnny's voice was thick with emotion.

Marcos swallowed down his rage. "We should have brought in more backup."

Johnny shook his head immediately. "No. This is personal."

Marcos glared at the man. "Yeah, but we need backup. This shit is high-tech, I thought the fucking Las Serpientes were some punk-ass street gang."

"Scared, Candela?" Devil taunted.

Marcos glared. "No. Just not fuckin' stupid," he shot back.

Devil's smirk turned into a sneer. The dim light played off the planes of his face, giving him a sinister air. "I'd like to see them once Mayhem gets a hold of 'em."

Marcos looked over at Johnny, who was already moving away from the group. "What's the plan?"

Johnny walked to the back of the van and pulled open the doors. "We go in, guns blazing," he called over his shoulder. He opened a heavy black cargo container that was about four feet by two by two. Marcos shook his head when Johnny popped the lid.

It was full of assault rifles.

"Well shit," Dagger breathed out.

"I knew you guys were into weapons...but damn," Stone muttered.

Marcos could only stare in disbelief. There would have been no way the Psychos could have won a war against the Ravager Knights. Buckley had been out of his mind. Marcos shook his head and moved in to grab a nine-millimeter tactical rifle. He checked the scope and smiled when he saw the LED sights. "Very nice," he muttered.

Kevin laughed, reaching over to switch something on, on the scope. A green LED laser was pointed inside the van. "No need to get fancy. Just aim and shoot tonight." Kevin nodded.

"Alright boys, let's roll out. We've got Welder and Hotrod on standby, but let's hope we don't need them," Johnny said and started walking away.

Devil and Rockstar chuckled and followed their leader.

Marcos shared a look with Stone and Dagger. Stone shook his head, and Dagger laughed softly before he reached for his own weapon. Dagger was a crazy bastard most days, so something like going in guns blazing was right up his alley.

Marcos pulled out his phone and sent a quick text to Axel with their address.

Marcos

Be prepared to back us up if needed.

Axel

Got it.

Simple and to the point. Axel would show up with Blaze and Phoenix and would wait until they were needed.

Thankfully Johnny had his own fail-safe in place, just in case.

The six of them were quiet as they stealthily circled the buildings. "My guy is in their feed and covering our tracks," Johnny muttered over his shoulder to Marcos. "Stay close to the building."

Johnny, Derrick, and Kevin moved as a unit, as if they had trained for this. Marcos assumed they probably had. The three of them had been special forces at one time, had done rescue missions like this one probably a hundred times.

Marcos had never served in the military; he hadn't wanted to be so far away from Kara. She needed him. He let Johnny and his guys take point and listened to their directions as they moved around the compound.

"Jack, the door's locked," Johnny muttered with a finger pressed to his earpiece.

Marcos didn't hear the response, but a moment later, Johnny tried the door again and it opened silently.

They entered a dimly lit warehouse. Pallets of boxes sat gathering dust in the large open space. Dark, narrow aisles went between the pallets, which were stacked taller than Marcos. "This way," Johnny muttered, turning left and staying against the wall instead of venturing into the maze of boxes.

They trudged along silently, looking down each and every aisle for anyone coming their way, rifles out in front of them. The warehouse was eerily quiet. When they reached another outside wall, they turned right and continued forward.

Up ahead, a light shone brightly in the darkness, spotlighting a metal stairwell that led down. Johnny paused, still in the ring of darkness, and held up a hand signal that Marcos assumed meant stop. They waited and watched as two guards armed with assault rifles came up the steps from the basement with their backs to them.

Johnny motioned toward an aisle, and the six of them moved swiftly and silently behind the cover of boxes. Marcos waited, his skin crawling, as quiet footsteps headed their way.

Johnny and Rockstar jumped into action as the two guards started to pass by. Both men were fast and lethal as they grabbed the men from behind and made quick and silent work of snapping their necks.

Marcos's mouth dropped open in shock as they lowered the dead silently to the ground and then pulled them down the aisle and away from the main alley. Johnny and Kevin stripped the guards of their assault rifles and radios, and then they were moving forward again.

Johnny leaned out, making sure the coast was clear, before he led the way toward the stairs again.

It amazed Marcos how silently the six of them moved, how quickly they managed to descend the stairs. Johnny pressed forward at the bottom, not even pausing to verify direction; he was being led via earpiece by his hacker, who was watching through the cameras.

As smoothly as they had been moving, things quickly turned to shit. A shot rang out from behind them, and Dagger cursed as he went down. "Fuck." He groaned, clutching his shoulder.

Marcos covered his brother and shot down the hallway toward the stairs they had come down, where two guards were moving quickly. Marcos shot once more, hitting one in the head just as the other one fell to the ground, shot by someone on his team.

"Are we good?" Johnny asked, moving toward Dagger.

"Fine," Dagger replied. "Keep moving. They know we're here now."

Johnny nodded once, and they moved on, running now that there was no more need to be quiet.

Marcos hung back a moment to check in with Dagger. "I'm fine. Go get her," Dagger said.

"Go," Stone told Marcos. "I'll stay with him."

Marcos nodded once and took off after Johnny and his boys. He hated leaving his own team behind, but his sister needed him. He needed to get to her. He only prayed they found her in time.

Chapter Twenty-Four

G UNSHOTS ECHOED IN THE distance.

Kara startled out of her meditative state, jostling her ribs and making her groan. She was sick of her body constantly being hurt. She needed to get up. She slowly uncurled, her ribs screaming in protest. The pain was an old friend at this point.

When she was flat on her back, she turned her head toward the door. Mr. Dead Eyes was still watching her, unblinking.

Gunshots echoed in the hall again, this time closer. She prayed it was her guys coming to save her. She never used to be one of those women who needed saving—she used to laugh about damsels in distress. But here she was hoping her men would come save her from this hell.

She rolled over onto her uninjured side and, using the move she learned in physical therapy, pushed herself into a sitting position just as the door banged opened. It flew against the concrete wall, and Kara gasped.

"Kara!" Johnny shouted as he led the way into the room.

Kevin was hot on his heels. He turned as he entered and saw Mr. Dead Eyes sitting there. Kevin shot twice before Mr. Dead Eyes even shifted his eyes from Kara. Two rounds, right in the chest.

Kara let out a small shriek as her captor fell sideways out of his chair.

"Baby girl, are you hurt?" Derrick rushed to her side as Johnny crouched before her.

She stared at the vacant expression in Mr. Dead Eyes's...dead eyes. Her heart beat uncontrollably, her hands shook, and she heard the blood rushing in her ears. She couldn't take her eyes off him. His empty gaze would be burned in her memory for the rest of her life.

Even in death, he still stared.

"Princess, we need you with us," Johnny's gruff voice said. Then his face was in front of hers, blocking her view of the man in the corner. "How badly are you hurt?" he asked.

Kara blinked and focused on Johnny's face. His blond hair was covered by a backward baseball hat, his blond beard was trimmed short, and his blue eyes were dark as they narrowed on hers. She reached out and ran her fingers down his cheek.

His eyes fluttered for a moment, as if they were going to close. Instead, he gently grabbed her fingers and held them in his own. "Kara," he said again, softly, "we need to move. How badly are you hurt?"

"My ribs are broken again," she muttered softly. Her voice was thick—she hadn't had any water in twenty-four hours, and her body ached everywhere.

"Can you walk?" Derrick asked from her right.

"I don't know," she murmured, feeling dazed.

"She's in shock," Kevin said from the doorway where he stood guard with Marcos. "Pick her up and let's move."

"Come here, baby girl," Derrick said softly, sliding his arms under her knees and behind her back. She wrapped her arm around his shoulders and clung to his shirt as he lifted her from the mattress.

Kara hissed in pain as her ribs were jostled.

Gunshots echoed in the distance again.

"We need to move now," Kevin ordered, his gaze roaming over Kara. "You good, baby?"

"Let's go." She nodded at him.

Kevin led the way out of her cell, his assault rifle held out in front of him. Johnny was right on his heels, Derrick following with Kara.

"Kara," Marcos muttered as they walked through the door. He was on their asses as they moved, gun out and covering them from behind.

"Hey, big brother," she murmured, suddenly feeling exhausted. She rested her head in the crook of Derrick's neck.

"Baby girl, I need you to stay awake just a little longer. Can you do that for me?" Derrick asked softly.

She murmured against his throat, but she was fading fast. "Shit." She heard Derrick curse as he held her tighter against him. It was the last thing she knew before everything went black around her.

Kara woke to an incessant beeping. A dull ache radiated throughout her body, though her knees and ribs burned the worst. There was a throbbing in her head, but it wasn't horrible.

She was finally warm. After unknown hours or days of shivering from the cold, she was finally warm. Blankets weighed her down, or was that someone lying on her? She shifted and blinked her eyes open.

The hospital room was dimly lit, but she could clearly see the men stationed around her room...and Kevin curled around her body in the hospital bed. Derrick was on her other side, holding her hand, his head resting on the bed, sound asleep.

She found Johnny at the foot of her bed in a similar position as Derrick. He was holding her ankle under the blankets, half in the chair, half on her bed, and also sound asleep.

The door opened and light from the hall poured in. She couldn't see the door past Kevin's shoulders, but she didn't have to wait to see who it was. Marcos moved around the side of the bed and her boys. He squeezed between Derrick and the wall and finally stood near Kara's head. "Hey lil *Manita*," he whispered, pressing a kiss to her forehead.

"Hey, Marquitos." She sighed.

"How you feeling?" he asked.

"Sore," she answered honestly. "Is the baby OK?"

"Baby is fine," Kevin mumbled next to her, his hand sliding over her belly on top of the blankets.

She laced her fingers together with his and squeezed. "You sure? Did they do an ultrasound?" she asked, her voice getting louder with her questions. "What about my ribs? Did they pierce my lungs again? Or hurt the baby? What about my blood pressure?" she asked.

Johnny and Derrick both shifted awake as she spoke.

"Doctor did an ultrasound, and our baby is doing great. Your ribs just cracked a little bit, nowhere near like before," Kevin answered. His hand rubbed her belly again, their fingers still interlaced.

"You were pretty severely dehydrated, and your blood pressure was really low, but after a couple hours here, your levels started coming up," Marcos added.

"How long have I been out?" she asked.

Johnny's hand squeezed her ankle, and she smiled when she saw his sleepy gaze on hers. "I dunno, most of the day?" he guessed, looking around at the clock. "We brought you in around midnight last night."

Kara didn't know what time it was, but it was dark outside the window behind Marcos, so she assumed she'd slept the day away.

"What happened, baby?" Kevin asked, his fingers squeezing hers.

She squeezed back. "I don't know...four guys came into the office. I tried to fight them off, but they stuck me with a needle, I think. I woke up in that room."

"Did they hurt you?" Derrick asked, his voice gravelly.

She squeezed his hand and shrugged. "Not really?" She took a steadying breath. "I was mostly left alone. That man...the one you killed," Kara turned to face Kevin, "he never left. He never moved, he just sat there and stared at me the whole time. Never blinking, always watching. That was the worst part of it." Tears choked her throat. She gasped as a sob shuddered out of her and pain pierced her ribs.

"Shhh," Kevin murmured against her temple. He pressed a kiss there and rubbed his hand gently over her belly.

She turned her head to his chest as sobs racked her body. The beeping in the room got louder, and then the door was opening.

"Kara, how we doing in here?" a female voice asked as she stepped into the room.

Kara ignored her and cried into Kevin's chest.

"Kara, I understand you're upset right now, but we need you to calm down if you can," the woman spoke again. Her voice was strong and steady.

Kara used her breathing technique, and gradually the beeping began to slow down to a more normal rate as her heartbeat settled down.

"That's better," the woman said.

Kara pulled away from Kevin and looked over to see a short, curvy woman with black hair and green eyes. She had sharp cheekbones and a cute little nose. She was fricken gorgeous. Her green eyes held compassion as she smiled down at Kara.

"Hi there. I'm your nurse, Jade. On a scale of one to ten, can you tell me where your pain is currently?"

Kara sighed and thought about it. "Six, seven," she answered honestly. Her ribs were burning.

"Mmm," Jade hummed. "Sir, I'm going to have to ask you to get out of the bed." She wasn't mean about it, just matter-of-fact, as she had a job to do.

Kevin sighed and pressed a kiss to Kara's temple.

Kara tried to hide the wince as he jostled the bed while climbing out.

Her boys all took a step away and let Jade do her job. The small woman moved around the bed and helped Kara into a sitting position. She took her vitals and entered her numbers into the computer. "Alright Miss Kara, I'm going to message the doctor that you're awake and put in an order for pain meds. How does food sound?" Jade asked.

Kara's belly gave a grumble in answer. "Amazing." She smiled.

Jade grinned and nodded. "I'll put in an order of chicken broth and crackers. If you're OK in an hour, we can order dinner."

Kara nodded slowly. She was exhausted, and she knew once the pain meds hit her, she wouldn't be eating dinner.

After Jade left, Kara turned to Johnny. "What happened with my father?"

Johnny ran a hand over his face and sighed. "We turned him over to the DA."

Kara could see the distress on his face. He hadn't wanted to. She knew that. She knew how it was eating him up inside to have given him up. She gave him a grateful smile. "Thank you." She nodded to him.

He nodded back at her.

"Thank you, all of you, for coming for me." She gasped, trying not to cry again.

"Baby girl," Derrick spoke. "There's no place on this planet, or in hell, that we wouldn't venture to get you back. We will *always* come for you."

Kara gave him a watery smile and reached out to him. She needed a kiss.

He smirked, then leaned down and kissed her slowly. Instead of the peck she was expecting, he sucked her bottom lip into his mouth and bit down gently.

She moaned, and her heart rate monitor started beeping faster.

The door opened while Derrick was still kissing her. "Am I going to have to ask you boys to leave?" Jade asked.

Kara giggled as she pulled away from Derrick. "No, ma'am, we'll be good."

Jade smirked. "Somehow I doubt that very much."

Soft laughter floated around the room and Kara sighed.

Jade walked out again, and Marcos shifted. "I'm gonna go check on Dagger," he said.

"What happened to Nico?" Kara asked.

"He was shot in the shoulder. He's in surgery," Marcos replied. He leaned down and pressed a kiss to her forehead. "I'll be back, lil *Manita*," he murmured.

Kara looked at her guys when her brother was gone and held out her hands. They immediately moved forward, positioning their chairs as close to her as possible and grabbing hands or her ankle again. "When can I go home?"

"Depends on the doctor," Kevin said, rubbing her hand.

"How were your ribs cracked?" Johnny asked softly, squeezing her ankle.

"I fought back. They tried moving me out of the room a couple times. The first time, I kneed one of the guys in the balls, and they backed off after choking me..." There was a chorus of cursing and growling from her men. She squeezed Derrick's and Kevin's hands. "The second time, I had been sleeping and one tried to grab me. I fought back. He punched me in the ribs..." Again, her men growled. She pulled her hands back so she could fidget with the blanket instead. "I told him I was pregnant, and he left me alone after that."

"We should have gone through there and wiped them all out," Johnny said, shaking his head.

"We still can," Derrick said darkly.

Kara's heart rate spiked, and the monitor started beeping loudly again.

The door opened and Jade walked in holding a tray of food. She had a stern expression on her face as she walked over to the rolling table and set the food down. "Alright friends, this is your last warning. Kara, you need to rest and stay calm. The boys will have to leave if we can't achieve that."

Kara sighed and nodded. "Can they stay the night if we behave?" she asked.

Jade frowned. "ICU rules state only one guest at a time, period."

Kara's heart rate spiked again, and Jade narrowed her eyes at the machine. "I need them to stay, all of them," Kara said softly.

Jade's green eyes softened in understanding. "Like I said, calm and rest and I didn't see anything."

"Yes, ma'am." Kevin smiled and nodded at the nurse.

Kara pulled the table closer and dug into her meager dinner. She hoped she could get real food soon, but judging by the size of the horse pills in a cup on the tray, she would be dozing off relatively soon.

Chapter Twenty-Five

MARCOS LET OUT A slow breath as he walked out of Kara's hospital room. She was alive, she was safe, and she was protected. It was more than he could ask for. His nerves were still rattled after the insane rescue mission they had performed.

He sent up a prayer of thanks to whomever was listening, thankful they had gotten out alive. He was also grateful Axel, Blaze, and Phoenix had been waiting on standby. In the end, they had needed not only the three of them as backup but also Welder and Hotrod.

They had killed many Las Serpientes and had gotten out with minimal damage. The van had been a lifesaver when it came to transporting both Kara and Dagger to the hospital. Kara had passed out shortly after Devil had lifted her into his arms, and Dagger was shot in the shoulder, unable to ride.

The doctor had been optimistic that the bullet hadn't nicked any of the major arteries in Dagger's shoulder, which was a miracle. But it had broken his clavicle into three pieces. It required extensive surgery to repair, so Dagger wasn't out of the woods just yet.

Marcos was just thankful his brother and sister were alive. He sighed and took a left down the hall. Kara had been set up in the ICU due to her severe dehydration and concerns for the baby. It had terrified the shit out of Marcos at first, but after seeing her awake, he could appreciate the caution.

He hit the stairs and headed up a floor to the surgical waiting room. Stone was camped out in a corner chair, his leg bouncing up and down. He looked fucking wrecked. "Any update?" Marcos asked.

Stone ran a hand over his short blond hair and shook his head. The man was usually quiet, so it didn't faze Marcos when he didn't speak.

Marcos nodded slowly. "Let's go out for a smoke. We've got hours of waiting still."

Stone didn't respond. He stood up and headed for the door, leaving Marcos to trail after his buddy.

They got turned around when they were leaving, took the wrong elevator or something, because they ended up walking through the emergency department on their way out for a cigarette. And it wasn't the waiting area of the ER—they were in the back where patients were being seen.

He felt like an ass when he saw all the sick and injured patients separated from each other by curtains. He was in his head as he turned a corner and slammed bodily into someone. "Shit." He swore as his arms came up, hands landing on a woman's upper arms to steady the poor person he almost ran over.

She let out a small gasp, and Marcos froze as he looked down at the woman in his arms. "Maya." Marcos gasped, holding her a little tighter as he looked her over in disbelief.

Maya Henderson was as beautiful as she had been the last time he saw her, some ten years ago—when she took a job in Chicago and put Creekton and Mourningside and all of their history in the rearview. Her curly golden-brown hair was streaked with blond highlights. Her amber eyes were wide, and her plump, pink lips were slightly parted. She was both stunning and slightly stunned, by the looks of it.

"Marc," she whispered, gazing up at him, her wide caramel-colored eyes looking him over. Her eyes shifted past him. "Jase," she gasped just as softly.

"Hey, Darlin'," Jason said, his voice a smooth drawl. Whether he was affected by her sudden appearance or not, he didn't let on.

Marcos watched as the smooth honey of Stone's voice slid over Maya and made her shiver, just like it always used to. "What are you guys doing here?" she asked, her eyes darting between the two of them.

"Dagger's in surgery," Marcos said softly. He realized he was still holding her upper arms and slowly released them, letting his hands slide down her forearms before he finally dropped them to his sides.

She shivered slightly and tucked a stray hair behind her ear. "Is he OK?" Maya asked, her eyebrows furrowed as concern tugged at her features.

"He'll be fine," Stone answered, giving nothing away.

Maya's eyelids fluttered slightly; his voice always got to her. For a man who didn't talk much, he used to have Maya eating out of the palm of his hand whenever he spoke softly to her.

"Mom!" a young boy's voice called out from behind the curtain at Maya's back.

Marcos looked over her shoulder through the half-open curtain and froze. There was a young boy who looked about ten years old, give or take, and he was the spitting image of Marcos at that age. The resemblance to Marcos, even now, was uncanny. He was a mini-Marcos.

"What the *fuck*?" Stone's voice was a crack in the silence, and even Marcos startled at his tone. Marcos stared at the kid in disbelief and awe. There was no doubt in his mind the child was his.

"How?" Marcos asked, not even sure what he was asking. He couldn't tear his eyes away from the kid.

The child in question was staring back at him with equally wide eyes. He had dark black hair and deep brown eyes that matched Marcos's. His left arm was in a sling, and he was lying back, propped up on the gurney.

"Mom," the kid called again.

Maya glanced at him and gave him a pained smile. "Just a minute, honey."

"Mom, I want to meet him," the boy said. His voice was gentle, still that of a boy, but it was steady and sure. He knew what he wanted.

Maya's eyes closed and she took a deep breath.

"Maya?" Marcos asked, needing to hear her say it.

"Would you like to meet your son?" she asked softly. She looked at his chest, unable to meet his gaze.

"I would love to meet my son," Marcos said. He didn't give Maya a chance to speak. He brushed by her without another word and walked into the curtained space.

The boy was small, but he had a determined expression on his face. "Hello." Marcos smiled easily at the boy. "I'm Marcos. What's your name?" He held out his hand in greeting.

"Hi," the boy said. He put his hand in Marcos's and maintained eye contact while he firmly shook it. Marcos was impressed. "I'm Lucas. My friends call me Luke."

"Hi Lucas. I'm sorry I didn't know about you before today," Marcos said, pulling a chair up to the bedside.

Lucas gave a faint smile. "Not your fault. You can call me Luke."

Marcos grinned and nodded. "Alright, Luke. How old are you?"

"Nine. My birthday is in three months. I'll be ten." He smiled.

"Almost double digits—that's a big deal."

"I know. I keep telling my mom I should get a phone," Luke said, shifting on the bed. He winced slightly, and Marcos frowned.

"A phone is a big deal." Marcos nodded. He vaguely heard Maya and Stone arguing in hushed tones behind him, but he didn't give a damn. "Maybe we can work on your mom together." He winked at his son. "How else am I going to be able to talk to my son?"

Luke beamed and nodded enthusiastically. When he winced again due to his own enthusiasm, he sighed.

"How'd you hurt yourself?" Marcos asked, trying to keep his voice light.

"I fell off the monkey bars," Luke answered, not meeting Marcos's eyes.

Marcos smirked at the blatant lie. "Fell, huh?"

"I might have jumped," Luke admitted. "Tommy Bradshaw dared me, and Jinny Thomas was watching, so I couldn't punk out."

Marcos didn't even try to hide the impressed laugh that escaped him. He vaguely wondered if he should put on some kind of parental air but decided against it. He wasn't this kid's dad regardless of the fact that he was probably his father. He would work on a friendship with the kid before anything else. "Nah, dude. You couldn't punk out," Marcos agreed.

Luke smiled brightly and shook his head.

"So what'd they say? Is it busted?" Marcos finally asked.

Luke nodded. "Yep. Broke my wrist. Doc said I don't need surgery, though. They're just backed up and need to get me upstairs to have a cast put on."

Marcos nodded thoughtfully. "My sister broke her wrist not too long ago," Marcos told him. "She had a bright pink cast. What color cast you gonna get?"

Luke's eyes widened. "I can pick the color?"

"Sure can." Marcos nodded.

He heard footsteps behind him before he heard someone new speak up. "Alright little dude," a man said. "Are we ready to get a cast on and get out of here?"

Marcos looked over his shoulder to see a bright-eyed older man dressed in scrubs and a white coat. Just past the doctor were Maya and Stone. Stone sported his usual inscrutable expression while Maya looked anxious, and her eyes were red rimmed like she'd been crying.

Marcos felt a pang of sympathy in his heart for her but chose to ignore it. She hadn't told him about his son for ten years. He was allowed to be upset.

Luke looked at the doctor, and for the first time Marcos saw the kid look scared. Maya moved past Marcos and reached for Luke's right hand. "We sure are, aren't we Luke?" She gave him a smile.

The kid surveyed his mother's face, seeing the pain there. Luke squeezed her hand and looked at the doctor. "Let's do this."

"That's what I like to hear. Why don't we push your bed up there and your parents can follow me. We'll head up to orthopedics on the second floor," the doctor said.

No one bothered to correct him.

Marcos let Maya go ahead of him while he hung back a moment in the hallway next to Stone. "And?" he asked his brother when Maya and Luke were out of earshot.

"Long story, brother," Stone grumbled and shook his head.

Marcos nodded slowly, watching Maya follow the doctor down the hall. Luke peeked around the doctor's shoulder, looking for Marcos to catch up. "I'm gonna stay with them for awhile. You head back up to Dagger, let me know when you hear anything."

Stone sighed and nodded. He turned and held his hand out. Marcos grabbed it and pulled Stone into a bro hug. Stone slapped him on the back before he squeezed his shoulder. "Be careful, brother." He nodded once.

Marcos patted Stone on the back before turning to look for Luke and Maya. She had stopped a couple feet behind Luke's bed, waiting.

Marcos followed after them, making the choice to follow his son and see where this would take him.

Chapter Twenty-Six

"Hey, lil *Manita*." Marcos smiled as he walked into the hospital room. "Ready to bust out of here?"

"YES!" Kara exclaimed, looking up from her cell phone. "They're driving me nuts." She waved absently at her men scattered around the room.

There were grunts in reply, but they were engrossed in their own phones or books, just as she had been. They all were bored to tears and dying to go home.

Marcos laughed. "Cranky, sister?" he asked, raising an eyebrow.

She rolled her eyes. "How's Dagger?" she asked, deflecting.

"He's good." He nodded and pulled up a chair next to her bed. Marcos rubbed a hand over his buzzed hair. "I ran into Maya yesterday," he said hesitantly.

Kara gasped and dropped her phone. "No fucking way! Where?"

"Downstairs in the ER." Marcos sighed. "She was here with her son."

Kara's hands flew to her mouth. "What the fuck?" she muttered, her eyes wide.

Marcos nodded slowly. "He's almost ten." He gave her a watery smile.

"Marquitos," she murmured softly. Her heart raced as her mind whirled a million miles an hour waiting for her brother to admit the truth.

Marcos nodded again. "I have a son."

Kara flew out of the bed and pulled her brother into a hug despite the pain in her ribs. His shoulders shook under her cheek as he silently sobbed against her. She hugged him tighter, ignoring her own pain. She held him until he calmed down and turned away from her, wiping his eyes. "Tell me everything," she murmured.

"His name is Lucas. He's almost ten, and he's amazing." Marcos shook his head with a smile. "Maya's parents aren't doing well, so she moved back here to help them. She's living in Mourningside. She said she's told him about me over the years, whenever he asked. She said he's wanted to meet me for awhile." He shrugged. "We exchanged phone numbers. Gonna take it day by day, I guess. I'm not walking away," he added vehemently.

Kara had to wipe the tears from her own face. She smiled at her brother. "I can't wait to meet him."

Marcos's smile was blinding. "Me too, sister. Me too."

"We should probably talk about what Buckley said at the end." Johnny spoke up a while later, after the conversation had moved away from Lucas to future plans.

"I wouldn't worry about the last words of a dead man." Marcos shook his head.

Johnny shook his head. "Nah man, it's not that. I found my father's journal. There was a lot of truth to what Buckley spouted.

Marcos tilted his head in question.

Johnny held up the leather-bound journal he had been reading. "King made a deal with the Seratellis to move their coke. It was recent. He didn't tell us. The move undercut a deal the Seratellis already had with the Psychos. So Buckley was right about the deal blowing up the coke trade from here to Alabama."

Marcos rubbed a hand over his buzzed head. Kara could see the stress he carried.

Johnny continued before Marcos could answer him. "The Knights have had a long-standing deal with the Bratva out of Chicago. We run drugs for the Tarazov family, sometimes weapons. We keep everything out of Mourningside and send it to Bloomington or Louisville, Birmingham, New Orleans."

"Keep it out of Mourningside and in Creekton?" Marcos asked, looking annoyed.

"It's not like that." Johnny shook his head, disagreeing. "The Seratellis do their own dealing, they have their own crews. We just move large quantities out of the area. Imagine the amount of product there'd be on the street if we didn't?"

Kara sighed. She really didn't like this kind of talk. She wished her boys were safe at all times and not at risk of being picked up by the ATF for fucking moving product across state lines.

Johnny locked eyes with Kara and nodded slowly. "I know, Princess, I know."

Kara shrugged, annoyed.

"We'll talk about it later," Johnny said to Marcos, holding up the journal again.

Marcos frowned and reached for the leather-bound book.

Johnny paused. "He, uh, also went into detail about you being his son and what he thought that would have meant when we were kids," he explained.

Marcos froze, arm halfway extended, and frowned. "Like he knew all along he was my father?"

"Not in the sense of who you were exactly, more that he suspected Carlita lied about the paternity test to stay with Vince for his money and that you were out there somewhere, another son of his," Johnny elaborated. "He never saw Carlita again after she told him Vince was the father."

Marcos was speechless as Johnny handed him the journal.

"You can have that." Johnny nodded toward the book.

"Thanks," Marcos said, tucking it into an inner pocket on his cut.

Kara smiled at her boys. After all the twisting turns life had thrown their way, she was glad for the peace between her brother and her guys. She was grateful they could get along and appreciated the fact that they all seemed to do it for her sake. Most of all, she was glad to have each and every one of them in her life and that they were all healthy and whole and together.

"Alright, Miss Kara." The jovial doctor grinned as he walked into the room, clipboard in hand.

Kara forced a smile. She'd been in the hospital two days now. She was hungry, exhausted, and irritated. She just wanted to go home and sleep in her own bed.

"I've got good news!" He beamed. "Discharge papers are right here. I passed your nurse on my way and let her know. She'll come help you pack up." He glanced around. Her boys had already packed up everything they had brought, which wasn't much since they hadn't even planned on being there this long.

The doctor chuckled a bit. "Alright, well in that case, I have one last thing, a gift if you want it." He smiled. "I have the blood test results. I can tell you the sex of your baby, if you'd like?"

"Yes!" All three of her guys shouted immediately.

Kara laughed. "Oh, I don't know." She hummed, looking over at her boys with a playful smirk. She could see their faces falling.

"Babe, puh-lease!" Kevin said, standing up from his chair and walking toward her.

"I'll get on my knees and beg if I have to," Derrick added, also walking over.

"You owe us," Johnny said, crossing his arms over his chest.

"Oh?" Kara snapped and crossed her arms over her chest. Leave it to Johnny to get her riled up. "How the fuck do I owe you?" she demanded.

Johnny smirked, knowing damn well he was getting under her skin. He fucking lived for it. He nodded as a smirk tugged at his lips. "For your father."

Kara rolled her eyes as understanding dawned on her. *Because I didn't let them kill my father.* She laughed and shook her head.

"Alright, Johnathan. You win, as always." She turned to the doc with a smile. "Let's hear it, Doc. What are we having?"

The doctor had a wide grin on his face when he glanced around the room and said, "It's a girl!"

Kara cracked up as, one by one, each of her men fell to their knees around her bed. Their astonished looks of disbelief would be forever burned into her brain.

They had a whole new life to look forward to, and Kara could not wait.

Epilogue

KARA LOOKED AROUND THE backyard at all the people she had come to love over the last year. The Ravager Knights mingled with the Devil's Psychos, old ladies mixed with some of her girlfriends from the office and college, kids ran around or were passed around from parent to parent.

Her men were not too far away, tossing bags in a game of cornhole.

Music played and laughter rang through the air. The scent of the roasting pig carried on the wind, making everyone hungry.

Kara had her feet propped up on a lounge chair, as her ankles were swelling in the unseasonably warm early spring. Her nephew

Lucas sat beside her talking a mile a minute. "Do you think we can go swimming after dinner?" he asked.

Kara laughed. "You don't have to wait until after dinner. Go now. Get the kids and go!" she suggested.

"Heck yes! Yo, Ryan!" Luke yelled and went chasing after a boy further out in the yard.

Maya laughed next to Kara. "They won't get out once they're in." She smiled.

Kara laughed. "Then maybe I'll get some peace and quiet."

"You won't." Maya shook her head, her smile in place. "They'll be screaming and roughhousing in three seconds."

Kara just grinned, loving every moment of having Luke around. "How are things with my brother?" she asked Maya.

The smile on Maya's face faltered slightly. Had Kara not been so practiced at reading people as a lawyer, she might have missed it. Maya's amber eyes weren't as bright as they had been. "They're...good," she said hesitantly.

Kara raised an eyebrow at her. "I think you forgot you're talking to a lawyer here."

"Trust me, girl, no one forgets that," Maya said, looking away.

Kara narrowed her eyes on the woman, cataloging every detail. Maya was only thirty-four years old, and while she looked great, she was also showing signs of stress. She had been taking care of her elderly parents after they'd been in a car accident. They were adjusting to life afterward and learning their capabilities with limited mobility, and they depended heavily on Maya.

"How are you doing, Maya?" Kara asked, changing tactics.

"I'm fine." Maya shrugged.

Kara shook her head. "Girl, I don't care if you and my brother never get back together...but don't shut me out, not again. Once upon a time we were close."

Maya's face fell, and she looked down. "I'm sorry. I know I'm being a pain in the ass," she said. "I'm not doing well." She shook her head, and golden-brown curls fell in her face. She absently tucked them behind her ear. "Being back here is hard. Seeing my parents the way they are...it's hard. It's just all so hard."

Kara took her hand in hers and squeezed. "Lean on us, girl. We've got you, whatever you need."

Maya swallowed and nodded. "I'm going to go check on Luke, make sure he found his swimsuit."

Kara let her go without another word. Maya and Marcos had a long road ahead of them. Kara was just glad that in the last six months, Maya had given Marcos unencumbered access to Luke.

Even Jason and Nico had taken a shine to the boy, but Marcos and Luke were like two peas in a pod. Kara had never seen her brother happier.

"How we doing over here, pretty momma?" Derrick asked as he rounded her lounge chair and pressed a kiss to the top of her head.

She smiled and looked up to find her three men standing around her. She had been so lost in thought she hadn't noticed they'd finished their game. "I'm good. How are my guys?"

"We would be better if you were naked." Kevin smirked down at her.

She rolled her eyes. "Should we just kick out all of our friends and family so we can go upstairs and fuck?" she asked.

"Sounds like a great plan, Princess." Johnny chuckled and leaned down. He pressed a kiss to her lips. "We don't have to kick them out, though. We could just sneak inside. No one would notice."

She laughed and kissed him again. "They would too notice. I'm the size of a house."

"A sexy house," Derrick joked.

Kara gave him the finger and kissed Johnny again. He was getting her riled up, but he might be on to something. "Help me up." She smirked.

Johnny grinned wickedly and grabbed her hands in his, pulling her to her feet.

She groaned as she felt an internal pull and then a snapping sensation, as if a rubber band inside her had snapped. There was a rush of warmth at the same time. "Oh fuck," she breathed out as she looked down.

"Did you just pee?" Luke asked, appearing in front of them dressed in his swim trunks.

"My water just broke." Kara gasped, eyes wide and locked on Johnny.

He laughed heartily and squeezed her hands. "Guess you're missing the pig roast, Princess."

"Baby time!" Derrick yelled, drawing attention.

Kara smacked his arm. "Thanks for calling attention, jerk."

"And so it begins." Kevin smirked. "How long until you're cursing us out and swearing you'll never have sex again?"

Kara ignored her boys and headed into the house. She wasn't in pain and had some time. She was going to shower and eat a meal before she had to leave.

She had the rest of her life to rush around. For now, she would take her time and enjoy the ride.

THE END

Loved the Ravager Knights and Devil's Psychos? Be on the look out for Marcos's story!

Brandishing Betrayals
A Devil's Psychos Book

Coming this summer! Release date to be determined!

Authors live for reviews! Please take a moment leave a review on amazon here!

Sign up for my newsletter here, for the latest updates and sneak peeks on what I'm working on.

Follow me on social media!

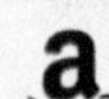

amazon.com/author/methornwood

facebook.com/methornwood

instagram.com/midnightdreamingwriting/

goodreads.com/author/show/45144764.M_E_Thornwood

tiktok.com/@me.thornwood.author

https://twitter.com/ME_Thornwood

Also By M.E. Thornwood

Did you miss out on Courting the Consequences?

Check it out here!

Choices have consequences, and some consequences cannot be undone.

Fighting to survive is all Kara Carmichael knows. Whether it was surviving the streets as a poor kid on the southside of Mourningside, Illinois or fighting the legal injustices in the court room, Kara prides herself on her ability to fight and win.

She also knows that every choice you make, has an outcome or consequence.

As the managing partner of the most prestigious law firm in the city, Kara had fought her way into a good life. She had made all the right choices.

Or so she thought.

When the Ravager Knights MC rolls into her law firm and kicks up trouble, Kara has a choice to make.

Fight the soul burning attraction of three rough and tumble bikers? Or fight for the prestigious job and gilded lifestyle she worked her entire life building?

Check out Reconciling the Consequences here!
Make a choice. Consequences be damned.

Kara made her choice, and the consequences of her choices left her burned and beaten.

After her father's hitman failed to kill her and her ex-boyfriend carried her body from the burning house, Kara wakes up in hospital... alone.

Without a home to return to, and her father still out for blood, Kara has only one choice left... beg for forgiveness from the three men whose hearts she deliberately broke. Or die trying.

Will Johnny, Derrick, and Kevin accept her apology and move on? Or will Kara have to face the consequences for her choices and save herself from her father?

Acknowledgments

OMG! Thank you to all my readers! To everyone that made to this point! Book 3 of my debut series! I published an entire series! Thank you so much for reading this! Its my dreams come true!

I wanna thank my husband for being incredibly supportive while I embark on this dream of mine. All the long hours you've put in with the kids and bedtimes, cooking dinner, and picking up my slack when I need to focus on meeting a deadline! I love you so much!

To Jessica Baker! This would not have been possible without you! Thank you so much for all you've taught me! You've answered every question I've had and given such great advice! Thank you so much.

To my bestie. My sister from another mister. I love you darling! We need a spa day!

To the bookstagram community for welcoming me with open arms and always being supportive. You guys rock!

Once again you readers, thank you so much for reading my books! I appreciate each and every one of you!

M.E. Thornwood is a contemporary Why Choose romance author that enjoys writing about dark themes, thrilling suspense, and hot hot spice. She loves her alpha males and the women who don't put up with them. Writing has been her passion since she was a little girl.

She lives in the Midwest with her husband and two children. When she's not writing, she's enjoying camping with family and friends, hiking with her kids, and reading books with her loveable fat cat Midnight.